"I love you," Tony said quietly.

Sharon's fork hung suspended. She remembered what the kids had said about the plans he'd made, and stiffened her spine. "Are you practicing for your hot date this weekend?" she asked.

"Jealous?"

"Not in the least," lied Sharon, jamming the fork into her rice as if it were a climber's flag she was planting on a mountain peak.

Tony caught her wrists and pulled until she was sitting on his lap. "Just this once," he suggested, his lips brushing against Sharon's, "let's skip the preliminary rounds, okay?"

"Okay," she whispered. She knew that what was about to happen was a mistake, but she couldn't stop it. The kiss was long and thorough and so intimate that it left Sharon disoriented. She was surprised to find herself lying on the floor, because she didn't remember moving. Tony's hand was unfastening her shirt when she stopped him. "This woman you're seeing this weekend—who is she?"

He kissed her again, playfully. "She's you," he answered. "If you don't turn me down, that is."

"Her characters come alive and walk right off the pages and into your heart."

—*Rendezvous*

LINDA LAEL MILLER

USED-TO-BE LOVERS

MIRA®

ISBN 1-55166-896-3

USED-TO-BE LOVERS

Copyright © 1988 by Linda Lael Miller.

All rights reserved. Except for use in any review, the reproduction or
utilization of this work in whole or in part in any form by any electronic,
mechanical or other means, now known or hereafter invented, including
xerography, photocopying and recording, or in any information storage or
retrieval system, is forbidden without the written permission of the publisher,
MIRA Books, 225 Duncan Mill Road, Don Mills, Ontario, Canada M3B 3K9.

All characters in this book have no existence outside the imagination of the
author and have no relation whatsoever to anyone bearing the same name
or names. They are not even distantly inspired by any individual known or
unknown to the author, and all incidents are pure invention.

MIRA and the Star Colophon are trademarks used under license and registered
in Australia, New Zealand, Philippines, United States Patent and Trademark
Office and in other countries.

Visit us at www.mirabooks.com

Printed in U.S.A.

For Jean and Ron Barrington,
living proof that romance is alive and well

1

Trying hard to concentrate on her work, Sharon Morelli squinted as she placed a wispy chiffon peignoir exactly one inch from the next garment on the rack. This was a standard antiboredom procedure reserved for days when almost no customers wandered into her lingerie shop, Teddy Bares. She was so absorbed in the task that she jumped when two dark brown eyes looked at her over the bar and a deep voice said, "Business must be slow."

Sharon put one hand to her pounding heart, drawing in a deep breath and letting it out again. Clearly, Tony hadn't lost his gift for catching her at a disadvantage, despite the fact that their divorce had been final for months. "Business is just fine," she snapped, hurrying behind the counter and trying to look busy with a stack of old receipts that had already been checked, rechecked and entered into the ledgers.

Without looking up she was aware that Tony had followed her, that he was standing very close. She also knew he was wearing battered jeans and a blue cambric work shirt open halfway down his chest, though she would never have admitted noticing such details.

"Sharon," he said, with the same quiet authority that made him so effective as the head of a thriving construction company and as a father to their two children.

She made herself meet his gaze, her hazel eyes linking with his brown ones, and jutted out her chin a little way. "What?" she snapped, feeling defensive. It was her turn to live in the house with Briana and Matt, and she would fight for that right if Tony had any ideas to the contrary.

He rolled his expressive eyes and folded his arms. "Relax," he said, and suddenly the shop seemed too small to contain his blatant masculinity. "We've got a project a couple of miles from here, so I stopped by to tell you that Matt is grounded for the week and Briana's with Mama—the orthodontist tightened her braces yesterday and her teeth are sore."

Sharon sighed and closed her eyes for a moment. She'd worked hard at overcoming her resentment toward Tony's mother, but there were times when it snuck up on her. Like now. Damn, even after all this time it hurt that Briana was Carmen's child and not her own.

Beautiful, perfect Carmen, much mourned by the senior Mrs. Morelli. Eleven years after her tragic death in an automobile accident, Carmen was still a regular topic of lament in Tony's extended family.

To Sharon's surprise, a strong, sun-browned hand reached out to cup her chin. "Hey," Tony said in a gentle undertone, "what did I say?"

It was a reasonable question, but Sharon couldn't answer. Not without looking and feeling like a complete fool. She turned from his touch and tried to compose herself to face him again. If there was one thing she didn't want to deal with, it was Maria Morelli's polite disapproval. "I'd appreciate it if you'd pick Bri up and bring her by the house after you're through work for the day," she said in a small voice.

Tony's hesitation was eloquent. He didn't understand Sharon's reluctance to spend any more time than absolutely necessary with his mother, and he never had. "All right," he finally conceded with a raspy sigh, and when Sharon looked around he was gone.

She missed him sorely.

It was with relief that Sharon closed the shop four hours later. After putting down the top on her yellow roadster, she drove out of the mall parking lot. There were precious few days of summer left; it was time to take the kids on the annual shopping safari in search of school clothes.

Sharon drew in a deep breath of fresh air and felt better. She passed by shops with quaint facades, a couple of restaurants, a combination drugstore and post office. Port Webster, nestled on Washington's Puget Sound, was a small, picturesque place, and it was growing steadily.

On the way to the house she and Tony had designed and planned to share forever, she went by a harborful of boats with colorful sails bobbing on the blue water, but she didn't notice the view.

Her mind was on the craziness of their situation. She really hated moving back and forth between her apartment and that splendid Tudor structure on Tamarack Drive, but the divorce mediators had suggested the plan as a way of giving the children a measure of emotional security. Therefore, she lived in the house three days out of each week for one month, four days the next, alternating with Tony.

Sharon suspected that the arrangement made everyone else feel just as disjointed and confused as she did, though no one had confessed to that. It was hard to remember who was supposed to be where and when, but she knew she was going to have to learn to live with the assorted hassles. The only alternative would be a long, bitter custody battle, and she had no legal rights where Briana was concerned. Tony could simply refuse to allow her to see the child, and that would be like having a part of her soul torn from her.

Of course he hadn't mentioned any such thing, but when it came to divorces, anything could happen.

When she reached the house, which stood alone at the end of a long road and was flanked on three sides by towering pine trees, Matt was on his skateboard in the driveway. With his dark hair and eyes, he was, at seven, a miniature version of Tony.

At the sight of Sharon, his face lighted up and he flipped the skateboard expertly into one hand.

''I hear you're grounded,'' she said, after

she'd gotten out of the car and an energetic hug had been exchanged.

Matt nodded, his expression glum at the reminder. "Yeah," he admitted. "It isn't fair, neither."

Sharon ruffled his hair as they walked up the stone steps to the massive front doors. "I'll be the judge of that," she teased. "Exactly what did you do?"

They were in the entryway, and Sharon tossed her purse onto a gleaming wooden table brought to America by some ancestor of Tony's. She would carry her overnight bag in from the trunk of the roadster later.

"Well?" she prompted, when Matt hesitated.

"I put Briana's goldfish in the pool," he confessed dismally. He gave Sharon a look of grudging chagrin. "How was I supposed to know the chlorine would hurt them?"

Sharon sighed. "Your dad was right to ground you." She went on to do her admittedly bad imitation of an old-time gangster, talking out of one side of her mouth. "You know the rules, kid—we don't mess with other people's stuff around here."

Before Matt could respond to that, Mrs. Harry, the housekeeper, pushed the vacuum across the living room carpet and then switched off the machine to greet Sharon with a big smile. "Welcome home, Mrs. Morelli," she said.

Sharon's throat felt thick, but she returned the older woman's hello before excusing herself to go upstairs.

Walking into the bedroom she had once shared with Tony was no easier than it had been the first night of their separation. There were so many memories.

Resolutely, Sharon shed the pearls, panty hose and silk dress she'd worn to Teddy Bares and put them neatly away. Then she pulled jeans, a Seahawks T-shirt and crew socks from her bureau and shimmied into them.

As she dressed, she took a mental inventory of herself. Her golden-brown hair, slender figure and wide hazel eyes got short shrift. The person Sharon visualized in her mind was short—five foot one—and sported a pair of thighs that might have been a shade thinner. With a sigh, Sharon knelt to search the floor of the closet for her favorite pair of sneakers. Her mind was focused wholly on the job.

A masculine chuckle made her draw back and swing her head around. Tony was standing just inside the bedroom doorway, beaming.

Sharon was instantly self-conscious. "Do you get some kind of sick kick out of startling me, Morelli?" she demanded.

Her ex-husband sat down on the end of the bed and assumed an expression of pained innocence. He even laid one hand to his heart. "Here I was," he began dramatically, "congratulating myself on overcoming my entire heritage as an Italian male by not pinching you, and you wound me with a question like that."

Sharon went back to looking for her sneakers, and when she found them, she sat down on the floor to wrench them onto her feet. "Where are the kids?" she asked to change the subject.

"Why do you ask?" he countered immediately.

Tony had showered and exchanged his work clothes for shorts and a tank top, and he looked good. So good that memories flooded Sharon's mind and, blushing, she had to look away.

He laughed, reading her thoughts as easily as he had in the early days of their marriage when things had been less complex.

Sharon shrugged and went to stand in front of the vanity table, busily brushing her hair. Heat coursed through her as she recalled some of times she and Tony had made love in that room at the end of the workday....

And then he was standing behind her, his strong hands light on her shoulders, turning her into his embrace. Her head tilted back as his mouth descended toward hers, and a familiar jolt sparked her senses when he kissed her. At the same time, Tony molded her close. Dear God, it would be all too easy to shut and lock the door and surrender to him. He was so very skillful at arousing her.

After a fierce battle with her own desires, Sharon withdrew, wide-eyed and breathless. This was wrong; she and Tony were divorced, and she was never going to be able to get on with her life if she allowed him to make love to her. "We can't," she said, and even though the words had been meant to sound light, they throbbed with despair.

Tony was still standing entirely too close, making Sharon aware of every muscle in his powerful body. His voice was low and practically hypnotic, and his hands rested on the bare skin of her upper arms. "Why not?" he asked.

For the life of her, Sharon couldn't answer. She was saved by Briana's appearance in the doorway.

At twelve, Briana was already beautiful. Her thick mahogany hair trailed down her back in a rich, tumbling cascade, and her brown eyes were flecked with tiny sparks of gold. Only the petulant expression on her face and the wires on her teeth kept her from looking like an angel in a Renaissance painting.

Sharon loved the child as if she were her own. "Hi, sweetie," she said sympathetically, able now to step out of Tony's embrace. She laid a motherly hand to the girl's forehead. "How do you feel?"

"Lousy," the girl responded. "Every tooth in my head hurts, and did Dad tell you what Matt did to my goldfish?" Before Sharon could answer, she complained, "You should have seen it, Mom. It was mass murder."

"We'll get you more fish," Sharon said, putting one arm around Bri's shoulders.

"*Matt* will get her more fish," Tony corrected, and there was an impatient set to his jaw as he passed Briana and Sharon to leave the room. "See you at the next changing of the guard," he added in a clipped tone, and then he was gone.

A familiar bereft feeling came over Sharon,

but she battled it by throwing herself into motherhood.

"Is anybody hungry?" she asked minutes later in the enormous kitchen. As a general rule, Tony was more at home in this room than she was, but for the next three days—or was it four?—the kids' meals would be her responsibility.

"Let's go out for pizza!" Matt suggested exuberantly. He was standing on the raised hearth of the double fireplace that served both the kitchen and dining room, and Sharon suspected that he'd been going back and forth through the opening—a forbidden pursuit.

"What a rotten idea," Bri whined, turning imploring eyes to Sharon. "Mom, I'm a person in pain!"

Matt opened his mouth to comment, and Sharon held up both hands in a demand for silence. "Enough, both of you," she said. "We're not going anywhere—not tonight, anyway. We're eating right here."

With that, Sharon went to the cupboard and ferreted out the supply of canned pasta she'd stashed at the back. There was spaghetti, ravioli and lasagna to choose from.

"Gramma would have a heart attack if she

knew you were feeding us that stuff,'' Bri remarked, gravitating toward another cupboard for plates.

Sharon sniffed as she took silverware from the proper drawer and set three places at the table. ''What she doesn't know won't hurt her,'' she said.

There were assorted vegetables in the refrigerator, and she assuaged her conscience a little by chopping enough of them to constitute a salad.

After supper, when the plates and silverware had been rinsed and put into the dishwasher and all evidence of canned pasta destroyed in the trash compactor, the subject of school came up. Summer was nearly over; D day was fast approaching.

Matt would be in the third grade, Briana in the seventh.

''What do you say we go shopping for school clothes tomorrow?'' Sharon said. Helen, the one and only employee Teddy Bares boasted, would be looking after the shop.

''We already did that with Gramma,'' Matt said, even as Bri glared at him.

Obviously, a secret had been divulged.

Sharon was wounded. She'd been looking forward to the expedition for weeks; she and the kids always made an event of it, driving to one of the big malls in Seattle, having lunch in a special restaurant and seeing a movie in the evening. She sat down at the trestle table in the middle of the kitchen and demanded, "When was this?"

Matt looked bewildered. He didn't understand a lot of what had been going on since the divorce.

"It was last weekend," Briana confessed. Her expression was apologetic and entirely too adult. "Gramma said you'd been under a lot of strain lately—"

"A lot of strain?" Sharon echoed, rising from the bench like a rocket in a slow-motion scene from a movie.

"With the shop and everything," Briana hastened to say.

"Quarterly taxes," Matt supplied.

"And credit card billings," added Briana.

Sharon sagged back to the bench. "I don't need you two to list everything I've done in the past two months," she said. Her disappointment was out of proportion to the situation; she realized that. Still, she felt like crying.

When Matt and Bri went off to watch television, she debated calling Tony for a few moments and then marched over to the wall phone and punched out his home number. He answered on the third ring.

Relief dulled Sharon's anger. Tony wasn't out on a date; that knowledge offered some comfort. Of course, it was early....

"This is Sharon," she said firmly. "And before you panic, let me say that this is not an emergency call."

"That's good. What kind of call is it?" Tony sounded distracted; Sharon could visualize his actions so vividly—he was cooking—that she might as well have been standing in the small, efficient kitchen of his condo, watching him. Assuming, that is, that the kitchen was small and efficient. She'd never been there.

Sharon bit down on her lower lip and tears welled in her eyes. It was a moment before she could speak. "You're going to think it's silly," she said, after drawing a few deep and shaky breaths, "but I don't care. Tony, I was planning to take the kids shopping for their school clothes myself, like I always do. It was important to me."

There was a pause, and then Tony replied

evenly, "Mama thought she was doing you a favor."

Dear Mama, with a forest of photographs growing on top of her television set. Photographs of Tony and Carmen. Sharon dragged a stool over from the breakfast bar with a practiced motion of one foot and slumped onto it. "I am not incompetent," she said, shoving the fingers of one hand through her hair.

"Nobody said you were," Tony immediately replied, and even though there was nothing in either his words or his tone to feed Sharon's anger, it flared like a fire doused with lighter fluid.

She was so angry, in fact, that she didn't trust herself to speak.

"Talk to me, Sharon," Tony said gently.

If she didn't do as he asked, Tony would get worried and come to the house, and Sharon wasn't sure she could face him just now. "Maybe I don't do everything perfectly," she managed to say, "but I can look after Briana and Matt. Nobody has to step in and take over for me as though I were some kind of idiot."

Tony gave a ragged sigh. "Sharon—"

"Damn you, Tony, don't patronize me!" Sharon interrupted in a fierce whisper, that might have been a shout if two children hadn't been in the next room watching television.

He was the soul of patience. Sharon knew he was being understanding just to make her look bad. "Sweetheart, will you listen to me?"

Sharon wiped away tears with the heel of her palm. Until then she hadn't even realized that she was crying. "Don't call me that," she protested lamely. "We're divorced."

"God, if you aren't the stubbornest woman I've ever known—"

Sharon hung up with a polite click and wasn't at all surprised when the telephone immediately rang.

"Don't you ever do that again!" Tony raged.

He wasn't so perfect, after all. Sharon smiled. "I'm sorry," she lied in dulcet tones.

It was after she'd extracted herself from the conversation and hung up that Sharon decided to take the kids to the island house in the morning. Maybe a few days spent combing the beaches on Vashon would restore her perspective.

She called Helen, her employee, to explain the change in plans, and then made the announcement.

The kids loved visiting the A-frame, and they

were so pleased at the prospect that they went to bed on time without any arguments.

Sharon read until she was sleepy, then went upstairs and took a shower in the master bathroom. When she came out, wrapped in a towel, the kiss she and Tony had indulged in earlier replayed itself in her mind. She felt all the attendant sensations and longings and knew that it was going to be one of those nights.

Glumly, she put on blue silk pajamas, gathered a lightweight comforter and a pillow into her arms and went downstairs. It certainly wasn't the first night she'd been driven out of the bedroom by memories, and it probably wouldn't be the last.

In the den Sharon made up the sofa bed, tossed the comforter over the yellow top sheet and plumped her pillow. Then she crawled under the covers, reaching out for the remote control for the TV.

A channel specializing in old movies filled the screen. There were Joseph Cotten and Ginger Rogers, gazing into each other's eyes as they danced. "Does Fred Astaire know about this?" Sharon muttered.

If there was one thing she wasn't in the mood for, it was romance. She flipped to a shopping network and watched without interest as a glamorous woman in a safari suit offered a complete set of cutlery at a bargain price.

Sharon turned off the television set, then the lamp on the end table beside her, and shimmied down under the covers. She yawned repeatedly, tossed and turned and punched her pillow, but sleep eluded her.

A deep breath told her why. The sheets were tinged with the faintest trace of Tony's aftershave. There was no escaping thoughts of that man.

In the morning Sharon was grumpy and distracted. She made sure the kids had packed adequate clothes for the visit to the island and was dishing up dry cereal when Tony rapped at the back door and then entered.

"Well," Sharon said dryly, "come on in."

He had the good grace to look sheepish. "I was in the neighborhood," he said, as Briana and Matt flung themselves at him with shouts of joy. A person would have thought they hadn't seen him in months.

"We're going to the island!" Matt crowed.

"For three whole days!" added Briana.

Tony gave Sharon a questioning look over their heads. "Great," he said with a rigid smile.

When the kids rushed off to put their duffel bags in the station wagon, the car reserved for excursions involving kids or groceries, Sharon poured coffee into his favorite mug and shoved it at him.

"I was going to tell you," she said.

He took a leisurely sip of the coffee before replying, "When? After you'd gotten back?"

Sharon hadn't had a good night, and now she wasn't having a good morning. Her eyes were puffy and her hair was pinned up into a haphazard knot at the back of her head. She hadn't taken the time to put on makeup, and she was wearing the oldest pair of jeans she owned, along with a T-shirt she thought she remembered using to wash the roadster. She picked up her own cup and gulped with the enthusiastic desperation of a drunk taking the hair of the dog. "You're making an awfully big deal out of this, aren't you?" she hedged.

Tony shrugged. "If you're taking the kids out of town," he said, "I'd like to know about it."

"Okay," Sharon replied, enunciating clearly. "Tony, I am taking the kids out of town."

His eyes were snapping. "Thanks," he said, and then he headed right for the den. The man had an absolute genius for finding out things Sharon didn't want him to know.

He came out with a payroll journal under one arm, looking puzzled. "You slept downstairs?"

Sharon took a moment to regret not making up the hide-a-bed, and then answered, "I was watching a movie. Joseph Cotten and Ginger Rogers."

Tony leaned back against the counter. "The TV in our room doesn't work?"

Sharon put her hands on her hips. "What is this, an audit? I felt like sleeping downstairs, all right?"

His grin was gentle and a little sad, and for a moment he looked as though he was about to confide something. In the end he finished his coffee, set the mug in the sink and went out to talk to the kids without saying another word to Sharon.

She hurried upstairs and hastily packed a bag of her own. A glance in the vanity mirror made her regret not putting on her makeup.

When she came downstairs again, the kids had finished their cereal and Tony was gone. Sharon felt both relief and disappointment. She'd gotten off to a bad start, but she was determined to salvage the rest of the day.

The Fates didn't seem to be on Sharon's side. The cash machine at the bank nearly ate her card, the grocery store was crowded and, on the way to the ferry dock, she had a flat tire.

It was midafternoon and clouds were gathering in the sky by the time she drove the station wagon aboard the ferry connecting Port Webster with Vashon Island and points beyond. Briana and Matt bought cinnamon rolls at the snack bar and went outside onto the upper deck to feed the gulls. Sharon watched them through the window, thinking what beautiful children they were, and smiled.

Briana had been a baby when her bewildered, young father had married Sharon. Sharon had changed Bri's diapers, walked the floor with her when she had colic, kissed skinned knees and elbows to make them better. She had made angel costumes for Christmas pageants, trudged from house to house while Briana sold cookies for her Brownie troop and ridden shotgun on trick-or-treat expeditions.

She had earned her stripes as a mother.

The ferry whistle droned, and Sharon started in surprise. The short ride was over, and the future was waiting to happen.

She herded the kids below decks to the car,

and they drove down the noisy metal ramp just as the heavy gray skies gave way to a thunderous rain.

2

Holding a bag of groceries in one arm, Sharon struggled with the sticky lock on the A-frame's back door.

"Mom, I'm getting wet!" Briana complained from behind her.

Sharon sunk her teeth into her lower lip and gave the key a furious jiggle just as a lightning bolt sliced through the sky and then danced, crackling, on the choppy waters of the sound.

"Whatever you do, wire-mouth," Matt told his sister, gesturing toward the gray clouds overhead, "don't smile. You're a human lightning rod."

"Shut up, Matthew," Sharon and Briana responded in chorus, just as the lock finally gave way.

Sharon's ears were immediately met by an ominous hissing roar. She set the groceries down on the kitchen counter and flipped on the lights as Bri and Matt both rushed inside in search of the noise.

"Oh, ick!" Bri wailed, when they'd gone down the three steps leading from the kitchen to the dining and living room area. "The carpet's all wet!"

Matt's response was a whoop of delight. His feet made a loud squishing sound as he stomped around the table.

"Don't touch any of the light switches," Sharon warned, dashing past them and following the river of water upstream to the bathroom. The source of the torrent proved to be a broken pipe under the sink; she knelt to turn the valve and shut off the flow. "Now what do I do?" she whispered, resting her forehead against the sink cabinet. Instantly, her sneakers and the lower part of her jeans were sodden.

The telephone rang just as she was getting back to her feet, and Matt's voice carried through the shadowy interior of the summer place she and Tony had bought after his family's company had landed a particularly lucrative contract three years before. "Yeah, we got here okay, if you don't count the flat tire. It's real neat, Dad—a pipe must have broke or something because there's water everywhere and the floor's like mush—''

Sharon drew in a deep breath, let it out again and marched into the living room, where she summarily snatched the receiver from her son's hand. "'Neat' is not the word I would choose," she told her ex-husband sourly, giving Matt a look.

Tony asked a few pertinent questions and Sharon answered them. Yes, she'd found the source of the leak, yes, she'd turned off the valve, yes, the place was practically submerged.

"So who do I call?" she wanted to know.

"Nobody," Tony answered flatly. "I'll be there on the next ferry."

Sharon needed a little distance; that was one of the reasons she'd decided to visit the island in the first place. "I don't think that would be a good idea..." she began, only to hear a click. "Tony?"

A steady hum sounded in her ear.

Hastily, she dialed his home number; she got the answering machine. Sharon told it, in no uncertain terms, what she thought of its high-handed owner and hung up with a crash.

Both Bri and Matt were looking at her with wide eyes, their hair and jackets soaking from the rain. Maternal guilt swept over Sharon; she started to explain why she was frustrated with Tony and gave up in midstream, spreading her hands out wide and then slapping her thighs in defeat. "What can I say?" she muttered. "Take off your shoes and coats and get up on the sofa."

Rain was thrumming against the windows, and the room was cold. Sharon went resolutely to the fireplace and laid crumpled newspaper and kindling in the grate, then struck a match. A cheery blaze caught as she adjusted the damper, took one of the paper-wrapped supermarket logs from the old copper caldron nearby and tossed it into the fire.

When she turned from that, Bri and Matt were both settled on the couch.

"Is Daddy coming?" Briana asked in a small voice.

Sharon sighed, feeling patently inadequate, and then nodded. "Yes."

"How come you got so mad at him?" Matt wanted to know. "He just wants to help, doesn't he?"

Sharon pretended she hadn't heard the question and trudged back toward the kitchen, a golden oasis in the gloom. "Who wants hot chocolate?'' she called, trying to sound light-hearted.

Both Bri and Matt allowed that cocoa would taste good right about then, but their voices sounded a little thin.

Sharon put water on to heat for instant coffee and took cocoa from the cupboard and milk and sugar from the bag of groceries she'd left on the counter. Outside the wind howled, and huge droplets of rain flung themselves at the windows and the roof. ''I kind of like a good storm once in a while,'' Sharon remarked cheerfully.

''What happens when we run out of logs?'' Briana wanted to know. ''We'll freeze to death!''

Matt gave a gleeful howl at this. ''Nobody freezes to death in August, blitz-brain.''

Sharon closed her eyes and counted to ten before saying, ''Let's just cease and desist, okay? We're all going to have to take a positive approach here.'' The moment the words were out of her mouth, the power went off.

Resigned to heeding her own advice, Sharon carried cups of lukewarm cocoa to the kids, then poured herself a mugful of equally unappealing coffee. Back in the living room, she threw another log on the fire, then peeled off her wet sneakers and socks and curled up in an easy chair.

"Isn't this nice?" she asked.

Briana rolled her eyes. "Yeah, Mom. This is great."

"Terrific," agreed Matt, glaring into the fire.

"Maybe we could play a game," Sharon suggested, determined.

"What?" scoffed Bri, stretching out both hands in a groping gesture. "Blindman's buff?"

It *was* a little dark. With a sigh, Sharon tilted her head back and closed her eyes. Memories greeted her within an instant.

She and Tony had escaped to the island often that first summer after they bought the A-frame, bringing wine, romantic tapes for the stereo and very little else. They'd walked on the rocky beaches for hours, hand in hand, having so much to say to each other that the words just tumbled out, never needing to be weighed and measured first.

And later, when the sun had gone and a fire had been snapping on the hearth, they'd listened to music in the dark and made love with that tender violence peculiar to those who find each other fascinating.

Sharon opened her eyes, grateful for the shadows that hid the tears glimmering on her lashes. *When did it change, Tony?* she asked in silent despair. *When did we stop making love on the floor, in the dark, with music swelling around us?*

It was several moments before Sharon could compose herself. She shifted in her chair and peered toward Bri and Matthew.

They'd fallen asleep at separate ends of the long couch and, smiling, Sharon got up and tiptoed across the wet carpet to the stairs. At the top was an enormous loft divided into three bedrooms and a bath, and she entered the largest chamber, pausing for a moment at the floor-to-ceiling windows overlooking the sound.

In the distance Sharon saw the lights of an approaching ferry and, in spite of her earlier annoyance, her spirits were lifted by the sight. Being careful not to look at the large brass bed she and Tony had once shared—Lord knew, the living room memories were painful enough—she took two woolen blankets from the cedar chest at its foot and carried them back downstairs.

After covering the children, Sharon put the last store-bought log on the fire and then made her way back to the chair where she rested her head on one arm and sighed, her mind sliding back into the past again, her gaze fixed on the flames.

There had been problems from the first, but the trouble between Tony and herself had started gaining real momentum two years before, when Matt had entered kindergarten. Bored, wanting to accomplish something on her own, Sharon had immediately opened Teddy Bares, and things had gone downhill from that day forward. The cracks in the marriage had become chasms.

She closed her eyes with a yawn and sighed again. The next thing she knew, there was a thumping noise and a bright light flared beyond her lids.

Sharon awakened to see Tony crouched on the hearth, putting dry wood on the fire. His dark hair was wet and curling slightly at the nape of his neck, and she had a compulsion to kiss him there. At one time, she would have done it without thinking.

''Hello, handsome,'' she said.

He looked back at her over one broad, denim-jacketed shoulder and favored her with the same soul-wrenching grin that had won her heart more than ten years before, when he'd walked into the bookstore where she was working and promptly asked her out. "Hi," he replied in a low, rumbling whisper.

"Have you been here long?"

Tony shook his head, and the fire highlighted his ebony hair with shades of crimson. "Ten minutes, maybe." She wondered if those shadows in his brown eyes were memories of other, happier visits to the island house.

She felt a need to make conversation. Mundane conversation unrelated to flickering firelight, thunderstorms, music and love. "Is the power out on the mainland, too?"

Again, Tony shook his head. There was a solemn set to his face, and although Sharon couldn't read his expression now, she sensed that his thoughts were similar to hers. When he extended his hand, she automatically offered her own.

"I'm hungry," complained a sleepy voice.

Tony grinned and let go of Sharon's hand to ruffle his son's hair. "So what else is new?"

"Dad, is that you?" The relief in the little boy's voice made Sharon wonder if she'd handled things so badly that only Tony could make them better.

Tony's chuckle was warm and reassuring, even to Sharon, who hadn't thought she needed reassuring. "One and the same. You were right about the floor—it is like mush."

Bri stirred at this, yawning, and then flung her arms around Tony's neck with a cry of joy. "Can we go home?" she pleaded. "Right now?"

Tony set her gently away. "We can't leave until we've done something about the flood problem—which means we're going to have to rough it." Two small faces fell, and he laughed. "Of course, by that I mean eating supper at the Sea Gull Café."

"They've got lights?" Bri asked enthusiastically.

"And heat?" Matt added. "I'm freezing."

"Nobody freezes in August," Bri immediately quoted back to him. "Blitz-brain."

"I see things are pretty much normal around here," Tony observed in wry tones, his head turned toward Sharon.

She nodded and sat up, reaching for her wet socks and sneakers. "An element of desperation has been added, however," she pointed out. "As Exhibit A, I give you these two, who have agreed to darken the doorway of the Sea Gull Café."

"It doesn't have that name for nothing, you

know,'' Bri said sagely, getting into her shoes. "Don't anybody order the fried chicken."

Tony laughed again and the sound, as rich and warm as it was, made Sharon feel hollow inside, and raw. She ached for things to be as they had been, but it was too late for too many reasons. Hoping was a fool's crusade.

Rain was beating at the ground as the four of them ran toward Tony's car. Plans encased in cardboard tubes filled the back seat, and the kids, used to their workaholic father, simply pushed them out of the way. Sharon, however, felt an old misery swelling in her throat and avoided Tony's eyes when she got into the car beside him and fastened her seat belt.

She felt, and probably looked, like the proverbial drowned rat, and she started with surprise when the back of Tony's hand gently brushed her cheek.

"Smile," he said.

Sharon tried, but the effort faltered. To cover that she quipped, "How can I, when I'm condemned to a meal of sea gull, Southern-style?"

Tony didn't laugh. Didn't even grin. The motion of his hand was too swift and too forceful for the task of shifting the car into reverse.

Overlooking the angry water, the restaurant

was filled with light and warmth and laughter. Much of the island's population seemed to have gathered inside to compare this storm to the ones in '56 or '32 or '77, to play the jukebox nonstop, and to keep the kitchen staff and the beaming waitresses hopping.

After a surprisingly short wait, a booth became available and the Morellis were seated.

Anybody would think we were still a family, Sharon thought, looking from one beloved, familiar face to another, and then at her own, reflected in the dark window looming above the table. Her hair was stringy and her makeup was gone. She winced.

When she turned her head, Tony was watching her. There was a sort of sad amusement in his eyes. "You look beautiful," he said quietly.

Matt groaned, embarrassed that such a sloppy sentiment should be displayed in public.

"Kissy, kissy," added Briana, not to be outdone.

"How does Swiss boarding school sound to you two?" Tony asked his children, without cracking a smile. "I see a place high in the Alps, with five nuns to every kid...."

Bri and Matt subsided, giggling, and Sharon felt a stab of envy at the easy way he dealt with them. She was too tired, too hungry, too vulnerable. She purposely thought about the rolled blueprints in the back seat of Tony's car and let the vision fuel her annoyance.

The man never went anywhere or did anything without dragging some aspect of Morelli Construction along with him, and yet he couldn't seem to understand why Teddy Bares meant so much to her.

By the time the cheeseburgers, fries and milk shakes arrived, Sharon was on edge. Tony gave her a curious look, but made no comment.

When they returned to the A-frame, the power was back on. Sharon sent the kids upstairs to bed, and Tony brought a set of tools in from the trunk of his car, along with a special vacuum cleaner and fans.

While Sharon operated the vacuum, drawing gallon after gallon of water out of the rugs, Tony fixed the broken pipe in the bathroom. When that was done, he raised some of the carpet and positioned the fans so that they would dry the floor beneath.

Sharon brewed a fresh pot of coffee and poured a cup for Tony, determined to do better than she had in the restaurant as the modern ex-wife. Whatever that was.

"I appreciate everything you've done," she said with a stiff smile, extending the mug of coffee.

Tony, who was sitting at the dining table by then, a set of the infernal blueprints unrolled before him, gave her an ironic look. "The hell you do," he said. Then, taking the coffee she offered, he added a crisp, "Thanks."

Sharon wrenched back a chair and plopped into it. "Wait one second here," she said when Tony would have let the blueprints absorb his attention again. "Wait one damn second. I *do* appreciate your coming out here."

Tony just looked at her, his eyes conveying his disbelief...and his anger.

"Okay," Sharon said on a long breath. "You heard the message I left on your answering machine, right?"

"Right," he replied, and the word rumbled with a hint of thunder.

"I didn't really mean that part where I called you an officious, overbearing—" Her voice faltered.

"Chauvinistic jerk," Tony supplied graciously.

Sharon bit her lower lip, then confessed, "Maybe I shouldn't have put it in exactly those terms. It was just that—well, I'm never going to know whether or not I can handle a crisis if you rush to the rescue every time I have a little problem—''

"Why are you so damn scared of needing me?" Tony broke in angrily.

Sharon pushed back her chair and went to the kitchen to pour a cup of coffee for herself. When she returned, she felt a bit more composed than she had a few moments before.

She changed the subject. "I was thinking," she said evenly, "about how it used to be with us before your construction company became so big—before Teddy Bares..."

Tony gave a ragged sigh. "Those things are only excuses, Sharon, and you know it."

She glanced toward the fire, thinking of nights filled with love and music. Inside, her heart ached. "I don't understand what you mean," she said woodenly.

"You're a liar," Tony responded with cruel directness, and then he was studying the blueprints again.

"Where are you sleeping tonight?" Sharon asked after a few minutes, trying to sound disinterested, unconcerned, too sophisticated to worry about little things like beds and divorces.

Tony didn't look up. His only reply was a shrug.

Sharon yawned. "Well, I think I'll turn in," she said. "Good night."

"Good night," Tony responded in a bland tone, still immersed in the plans for the next project.

Sharon fought an utterly childish urge to spill her coffee all over his blueprints and left the table. Halfway up the stairs, she looked back and saw that Tony was watching her.

For a moment she froze in the grip of some unnamed emotion passing between them, but her paralysis was broken when Tony dropped his gaze to his work.

Upstairs, Sharon took a quick shower, brushed her teeth, pulled on a cotton nightgown and crawled into the big, lonely bed. Gazing up at the slanted ceilings and blinking back tears of frustration, she wriggled down under the covers and ordered herself to sleep.

But instead of dreaming, Sharon reviewed the events of the evening and wondered why she couldn't talk to Tony anymore. Each time she tried, she ended up baiting him, or sliding some invisible door closed between them, or simply running away.

She was painfully conscious of his nearness and of her need for him, which had not been assuaged by months of telling herself that the relationship was over. She put one hand over her mouth to keep from calling his name.

From downstairs she heard the low but swelling strains of familiar music. Once, the notes had rippled over her like the rays of the sun on a pond, filling her with light. They had flung her high on soaring crescendos, even as she clung to Tony and cried out in passion....

Sharon burrowed beneath the covers and squeezed her eyes shut and, an eternity later, she slept. When she awakened the room was filled with sunlight and the scent of fresh coffee.

After a long, leisurely stretch, Sharon opened her eyes. A dark head rested on the pillow beside hers, and she felt a muscular leg beneath the softness of her thigh.

"Oh, God," she whispered, "we made love and I missed it!"

A hoarse laugh sounded from the pillow. "No such luck," Tony said. "Our making love, I mean. We didn't."

Sharon sat up, dragging the sheets up to cover her bosom even though she was wearing a modest cotton nightgown. She distinctly remembered putting it on, and with a quick motion of her hands, she lifted the sheet just far enough away from her body that she could check. The night-gown was still in evidence.

"What the devil do you think you're doing, Tony Morelli?" she demanded furiously.

He rolled onto his back, not even bothering to open his eyes, and simultaneously pulled the covers up over his face, muttering insensibly all the while.

"You guys made up, huh?" Briana asked from the doorway. She was all smiles and carrying two cups of coffee, hence the delicious aroma.

"No, we didn't," Sharon said primly.

"Not a very diplomatic answer," Tony observed from beneath the covers. "Now, she's going to ask— "

"Then how come you're in bed together?" the child demanded.

"See?" said Tony.

Sharon elbowed him hard, and crimson color flooded her face. "I don't know," she said with staunch conviction.

Briana brought the coffee to the end table on Sharon's side of the bed, and some of it slopped over when she set the cups down. There were tears brimming in her eyes.

"Damn you, Tony," Sharon whispered, as though there were no chance of Bri's not hearing what she said. "Explain this to her—right now!"

With a groan, Tony dramatically fought his way out from under the blankets and sat up. "There's only one bed," he said reasonably, running a hand through his rumpled hair and then yawning again. "The couch is too short for me, so I just crawled in with your mom."

"Oh," Bri said grudgingly, and left the room, shutting the door behind her.

"She didn't understand," Sharon lamented.

Tony reached past her to collect one of the cups of coffee. "Kids don't need to understand everything," he said.

If the man hadn't been holding a steaming hot cup of coffee, Sharon would have slapped him. As it was, she glared at him and stretched out a hand for her own cup.

After a while Tony got up and wandered into the adjoining bathroom, and Sharon didn't look to see whether or not he was dressed. When he returned, he crawled back into bed with her, rolling over so that one of his legs rested across both of hers.

His mouth descended toward hers, smelling of toothpaste, and he was definitely not dressed.

"Tony, don't—"

The kiss was warm, gentle and insistent. Sharon trembled as all the familiar sensations were awakened, but she also braced both hands against Tony's chest and pushed.

The motion didn't eliminate all intimate contact—Tony had shifted his weight so that he was resting lightly on top of her—but it did make it possible to speak.

"No," Sharon said clearly.

Tony slid downward, kissing her jawline, the length of her neck, her collarbone.

"No," she repeated with less spirit.

His lips trailed across her collarbone and then downward. He nibbled at her breast through the thin fabric of her nightgown.

Her voice was a whimper. "No," she said for the third time.

Tony's mouth came to hers; his tongue traced the outline of her lips. "You don't mean that," he told her.

Sharon was about to admit he was right when

there was a knock at the door and Bri called out in sunny tones, "Breakfast is served!"

Tony was sitting up, both hands buried in his hair, when Briana and Matt entered the room carrying trays.

3

The downstairs carpets were far from dry. "Leave the fans on for another day or so," Tony said distantly. Standing beside the dining room table, he rolled up a set of plans and slid it back inside its cardboard cylinder.

A sensation of utter bereftness swept over Sharon, even though she knew it was best that he leave. The divorce was final; it was time for both of them to let go. She managed a smile and an awkward, "Okay—and thanks."

The expression in Tony's eyes was at once angry and forlorn. He started to say something and then stopped himself, turning away to stare out the window at Bri and Matt, who were chasing each other up and down the stony beach. Their laughter rang through the morning sunshine, reminding Sharon that some people still felt joy.

She looked down at the floor for a moment,

swallowed hard and then asked, "Tony, are you happy?"

The powerful shoulders tensed beneath the blue cambric of his shirt, then relaxed again. "Are you?" he countered, keeping his back to her.

"No fair," Sharon protested quietly. "I asked first."

Tony turned with a heavy sigh, the cardboard cylinder under his arm. "I used to be," he said. "Now I'm not sure I even know what it means to be happy."

Sharon's heart twisted within her; she was sorry she'd raised the question. She wanted to say something wise and good and comforting, but no words came to her.

Tony rounded the table, caught her chin gently in his hand and asked, "What happened, Sharon? What the hell happened?"

She bit her lip and shook her head.

A few seconds of silent misery passed, and then Tony sighed again, gave Sharon a kiss on the forehead and walked out. Moving to the window, she blinked back tears as she watched him saying goodbye to the kids. His words echoed in her mind and in her heart. *What the hell happened?*

Hugging herself, as though to hold body and soul together, Sharon sniffled and proceeded to the kitchen, where she refilled her coffee cup. She heard Tony's car start and gripped the edge of the counter with one hand, resisting an urge to run outside, to call his name, to beg him to stay.

She only let go of the counter when his tires bit into the gravel of the road.

"Are you all right, Mom?" Bri's voice made Sharon stiffen.

She faced this child of her spirit, if not her body, with a forced smile. "I'm fine," she lied, thinking that Bri looked more like Carmen's photographs with every passing day. She wondered if the resemblance ever grieved Tony and wished that she had the courage to ask him.

"You don't look fine," Briana argued, stepping inside the kitchen and closing the door.

Sharon had to turn away. She pretended to be busy at the sink, dumping out the coffee she'd just poured, rinsing her cup. "What's Matt doing?"

"Turning over rocks and watching the sand crabs scatter," Bri answered. "Are we going fishing?"

The last thing Sharon wanted to do was sit at

the end of the dock with her feet dangling, baiting hooks and reeling in rock cod and dogfish, when right now her inclinations ran more toward pounding her pillow and crying. Such indulgences, however, are denied to mothers on active duty. "Absolutely," she said, lifting her chin and straightening her shoulders before turning to offer Bri a smile.

The child looked relieved. "I'll even bait your hooks for you," she offered.

Sharon laughed and hugged her. "You're one kid in a thousand, pumpkin," she said. "How did I get so lucky?"

Carmen's flawless image, smiling her beauty-queen smile, loomed in her mind, and it was as though Tony's first wife answered, "I died, that's how. Where would you be if it weren't for that drunk driver?"

Sharon shuddered, but she was determined to shake off her gray mood. In just two days she would have to give Briana and Matt back to Tony and return to her lonely apartment; she couldn't afford to sit around feeling sorry for herself. The time allowed her was too fleeting, too precious.

She found fishing poles and tackle in a closet, and Bri rummaged through the freezer for a package of herring, bought months before in a bait shop.

When they joined Matt outside, and the three of them had settled themselves at the end of the dock, Bri was as good as her word. With a deftness she'd learned from Tony, she baited Sharon's hook.

In truth, Sharon wasn't as squeamish about the task as Bri seemed to think, but she didn't want to destroy the child's pleasure in being helpful. "Thanks," she said. "I'm sure glad I didn't have to do that."

"Women," muttered Matt, speaking from a seven-year pinnacle of life experience.

Sharon bit back a smile. "Shall I give my standard lecture on chauvinism?" she asked.

"No," Matt answered succinctly. It was the mark of a modern kid, his mother guessed, knowing what a word like *chauvinism* meant.

Bri looked pensive. "Great-gramma still eats in the kitchen," she remarked. "Like a servant."

Sharon chose her words carefully. Tony's grandmother had grown up in Italy and still spoke almost no English. Maybe she followed the old traditions, but the woman had raised six children to productive adulthood, among other accomplishments, and she deserved respect. "Did you know that she was only sixteen years old when she first came to America? She didn't speak or understand English, and her marriage to your great-grandfather had been arranged for her. Personally, I consider her a very brave woman."

Bri bit her lower lip. "Do you think my mother was brave?"

Questions like that, although they came up periodically, never failed to catch Sharon off guard. She drew in a deep breath and let it out again. "I never met her, sweetheart—you know that. Wouldn't it be better to ask your dad?"

"Do you think he loved her?"

Sharon didn't flinch. She concentrated on keeping her fishing pole steady. "I know he did. Very much."

"Carl says they only got married because my mom was pregnant with me. His mother remembers."

Carl was one of the cast of thousands that made up the Morelli family—specifically, a second or third cousin. And a pain in the backside.

"He doesn't know everything," Sharon said, wondering why these subjects never reared their heads when Tony was around to field them. "And neither does his mother."

Sharon sighed. God knew, Tony was better at things like this—a born diplomat. He and Carmen would have made quite a pair. There probably would have been at least a half dozen more children added to the clan, and it seemed certain that no divorce would have goofed up the entries in the family Bible. Maria Morelli had shown her all those names, reaching far back into the past.

Sharon was getting depressed again. Before Bri could bring up another disquieting question, however, the fish started biting. Bri caught two, Matt reeled in a couple more, and then it was time for lunch.

The telephone rang as Sharon was preparing sandwiches and heating canned soup.

"It's Gramma!" Matt shouted from the front room.

"Tell her your dad isn't here," Sharon replied pleasantly.

"She wants to talk to you."

Sharon pushed the soup to a different burner, wiped her hands on a dish towel and went staunchly to the telephone. "Hello," she said in sunny tones.

"Hello, Sharon," Maria responded, and there was nothing in her voice that should have made her difficult to talk to.

All the same, for Sharon, she was. "Is there something I can help you with?"

"Michael's birthday is next week," Maria said. She was referring to her youngest son; Tony was close to him and so were the kids.

Sharon had forgotten the occasion. "Yes," she agreed heartily.

"We're having a party, as usual," Maria went on. "Of course, Vincent and I would like the children to be there."

Sharon's smile was rigid; her face felt like part of a totem pole. She wondered why she felt called upon to smile when Maria obviously couldn't see her.

A few hasty calculations indicated that Bri and Matt would have been with Tony on Michael's birthday anyway. "No problem," Sharon said generously.

There was a pause, and then Maria asked, "How are you, dear? Vincent and I were just saying that we never see you anymore."

Sharon rubbed her eyes with a thumb and a forefinger, suppressing an urge to sigh. She regarded Vincent as a friend—he was a gentle, easygoing man—but with Maria it seemed so important to say and do the right things. Always. "I-I'm fine, thanks. I've been busy with the shop," she responded at last. "How are you?"

Maria's voice had acquired a cool edge. "Very well, actually. I'll just let you get back to whatever it was that you were doing, Sharon. Might I say hello to Bri, though?"

"Certainly," Sharon replied, relieved to hold the receiver out to the girl, who had been cleaning fish on the back porch. "Your grandmother would like to speak with you, Briana."

Bri hastened to the sink and washed her hands, then reached eagerly for the receiver. The depth of affection this family bore for its members never failed to amaze Sharon, or to remind her that she was an outsider. Even during the happiest years she and Tony had shared, she'd always felt like a Johnny-come-lately.

"Hi, Gramma!" Bri cried, beaming. "I caught two fish and the floors got all flooded and this morning I thought things were okay between Dad and Mom because they slept together...."

Mortified, Sharon turned away to hide her flaming face. *Oh, Bri,* she groaned inwardly, *of all the people you could have said that to, why did it have to be Maria?*

"Right," Briana went on, as her words became clear again. "We're having—" she craned her neck to peer into the pan on the stove "—chicken noodle soup. Yeah, from a can."

Sharon shook her head.

"Listen, Gramma, there's something I need to know."

An awful premonition came over Sharon; she whirled to give Bri a warning look, but it was too late.

"Was my mother pregnant when she married my dad?"

"Oh, God," Sharon moaned, shoving one hand into her hair.

Bri was listening carefully. "Okay, I will," she said at last in perfectly ordinary tones. "I love you, too. Bye."

Sharon searched the beautiful, earnest young face for signs of trauma and found none. "Well," she finally said, as Bri brought in the fish but left the mess on the porch, "what did she say?"

"The same thing you did," Briana responded with a shrug. "I'm supposed to ask Dad."

Sharon allowed her face to reveal nothing, though Tony had long since told her about his tempestuous affair with Carmen and the hasty marriage that had followed. She had always imagined that relationship as a grand passion, romantic and beautiful and, of course, tragic. It was one of those stories that would have been wonderful if it hadn't involved real people with real feelings. She turned back to the soup, ladling it into bowls.

"I guess I could call him."

Sharon closed her eyes for a moment. "Bri, I think this is something that would be better discussed in person, don't you?"

"You *know* something!" the girl accused, coming inside and shutting the door.

"Wash your hands again, please," Sharon hedged.

"Dad told you, didn't he?" Briana asked, though she obediently went to the sink to lather her hands with soap.

Sharon felt cornered, and for a second or two she truly resented Bri, as well as Carmen and Tony. "Will you tell me one thing?" she demanded a little sharply, as Matt crept into the kitchen, his eyes wide. "Why didn't this burning desire to know strike you a few hours ago, when your father was still here?"

Briana was silent, looking down at the floor.

"That's what I thought." Sharon sighed.

"Listen, if it's too hard for you to bring this up with your dad, and you feel like you need a little moral support, I'll help. Okay?"

Bri nodded.

That afternoon the clouds rolled back in and the rain started again. Once more, the power went out. Sharon and the kids played Parcheesi as long as the light held up, then roasted hot dogs in the fireplace. The evening lacked the note of festivity that had marked the one preceding it, despite Sharon's efforts, and she was almost relieved when bedtime came.

Almost, but not quite. The master bedroom, and the bed itself, bore the intangible but distinct impression Tony seemed to leave behind him wherever he went. When Sharon retired after brushing her teeth and washing her face in cold water, she huddled on her side of the bed, miserable.

Sleep was a long time coming, and when it arrived, it was fraught with dreams. Sharon was back at her wedding, wearing the flowing white dress she had bought with her entire savings, her arm linked with Tony's.

"Do you take this man to be your lawful wedded husband?" the minister asked.

Before Sharon could answer, Carmen appeared, also wearing a wedding gown, at Tony's other side. "I do," Carmen responded, and Sharon felt herself fading away like one of TV's high-tech ghosts.

She awakened with a cruel start, the covers bunched in her hands, and sank back to her pillows only after spending several moments groping for reality. It didn't help that the lamp wouldn't work, that rain was beating at the roof and the windows, that she was so very alone.

The following day was better; the storm blew over and the electricity stayed on. Sharon made sure she had a book on hand that night in case her dreams grew uninhabitable.

As it happened, Carmen didn't haunt her sleep again, but neither did Tony. Sharon awakened feeling restless and confused, and it was almost a relief to lock up the A-frame and drive away early that afternoon.

The big Tudor house was empty when they reached it; Mrs. Harry had done her work and gone home, and there was no sign of Tony. The little red light on the answering machine, hooked up to the telephone in the den, was blinking rapidly.

Sharon was tempted to ignore it, but in the end she rewound the tape and pushed the Play button. Tony's voice filled the room. "Hi, babe. I'm glad you're home. According to Mama mia, I need to have a talk with Bri— I'll take care of that after dinner tonight, so don't worry about it. See you later." The tape was silent for a moment, and then another call was playing, this one from her mother. "Sharon, this is Bea. Since you don't answer over at the other place, I figured I'd try and get you here. Call me as soon as you can. Bye."

The other messages were all for Tony, so Sharon rewound the tape and then dialed her mother's number in Hayesville, a very small town out on the peninsula.

Bea answered right away, and Sharon sank into the chair behind Tony's desk. "Bea, it's me. Is anything wrong?"

"Where are you?" Bea immediately countered.

"At the house," Sharon replied in even tones.

"Crazy arrangement," Bea muttered. She had never approved of Sharon's marriage, Sharon's house or, for that matter, Sharon herself. "In, out, back, forth. I don't know how you stand it. Furthermore, it isn't good for those kids."

"Bea!"

"All right, all right. I just wanted to know if you were still coming over this weekend."

Sharon shoved a hand through her hair. She hated avoiding her own mother, but an encounter with Bea was more than she could face in her present state of mind. "I don't remember telling you that I'd be visiting," she said carefully, feeling her way along.

It turned out that Bea was suffering from a similar lack of enthusiasm. "It isn't like I don't want you to come or anything," she announced in her blunt way, "but Saturday's the big all-day bingo game, and one of the prizes is a car."

Sharon smiled to herself. "I see. Well, I have inventory at the shop, anyway. Call me if you win, okay?"

"Okay," Bea replied, but it was clear from her tone that her attention was already wandering. She was a beautician by trade, with a shop of her own, and an avid bingo player by choice, but motherhood had descended on her by accident. Bea Stanton had never really gotten the knack of it. "Part of the mill burned down," she added as an afterthought.

Sharon's father, who had never troubled to marry Bea, and probably would have been refused if he had proposed, was a member of the

Harrison family, which owned the mill in question. Hence Bea's assumption that Sharon would be interested.

"That's too bad," she said. "Was anybody hurt?"

"No," Bea answered distractedly. "There's one of those televisions that has a VCR built right in, too. At bingo, I mean."

"Good," Sharon answered, as a headache began under her left temple and steadily gained momentum. "If there's nothing else, Bea, I think I'd better hang up. I have to get the kids squared away before I go back to the apartment."

Bea started muttering again. Sharon said a hasty goodbye and hung up, and when she turned in the swivel chair, Tony was standing in the doorway.

She gasped and laid one hand to her heart. "I really wish you wouldn't do that!"

"Do what?" Tony asked innocently, but his eyes were dancing. He left the doorway to stride over and sit on the edge of the desk.

He was wearing dirty work clothes, but Sharon still found him damnably attractive.

"That was my mother," she said, in an effort to distract herself.

Tony's smile was slow, and he was watching

Sharon's lips as though their every motion fascinated him. "I hope you gave her my fondest regards."

"You don't hope any such thing," Sharon scoffed, scooting the chair back a few more inches.

Tony stopped its progress by bending over and grasping the arms in his hands. "I've missed you," he said, and his mouth was so close to hers that Sharon could feel his breath whispering against her skin.

"The kids are here," she reminded him.

He touched her lips with his and a sweet jolt went through her. One of his index fingers moved lightly down the buttoned front of her flannel shirt.

"Stop it," she said in anguish.

Tony drew her onto her feet and into his kiss, holding her so close that she ached with the awareness of his masculinity and his strength. She was dazed when, after a long interlude, the contact was broken.

In another minute she was not only going to be unable to resist this man, she could end up taking him by the hand and leading him upstairs to bed. Resolutely, Sharon stepped back out of his embrace. "Why, Tony?" she asked reasonably. "Why, after all these months, has it suddenly become so important to you to seduce me?"

He folded his arms across his chest. "Believe me," he said, "it isn't sudden. Has it ever occurred to you, Sharon, that our divorce might have been a mistake?"

"No," Sharon lied.

Tony's expression said he saw through her. "Not even once?" When she shook her head, Tony laughed. The sound was sad, rueful. "I've always said you were stubborn, my love."

Sharon was easing toward the door. "You'll talk to Bri?"

"I said I would," Tony replied quietly, his arms still folded, that broken look lingering in his eyes.

She cleared her throat. "Did your mother tell you what the problem is?"

Tony nodded. He looked baffled now, and watchful, as though he was curious about something. "I'm surprised it didn't come up before this, given the gossip factor. Sharon—"

She felt behind her for the doorknob and held on to it as though it could anchor her somehow. "What?"

"It bothers you, doesn't it? That Carmen was pregnant when I married her."

It would be stupid, and very uneighties, to be bothered by something like that, Sharon reasoned to herself. "Of course it doesn't," she said brightly, throwing in an airy shrug for good measure.

A look of fury clouded Tony's face, and in the next second he brought his fist down hard on the surface of the desk and rasped a swear-word.

Sharon's eyes were wide. She opened her mouth and then closed it again as Tony shook his finger at her.

"Don't lie to me," he warned in a low, even voice.

Sharon stepped inside the den and closed the door so that the kids wouldn't hear. "Okay," she whispered angrily, "you win. Yes, it bothers me that Carmen was pregnant! It bothers me that she ever existed! Are you satisfied?"

He was staring at her. "You were jealous of Carmen?" he asked, sounding amazed.

Sharon turned away to hide the tears she wasn't sure she'd be able to hold back, and let her forehead rest against the door. For several seconds she just stood there, breathing deeply and trying to compose herself. When she felt Tony's hands on her shoulders, strong and gentle, she stiffened.

His chin rested against the back of her head; she was aware of the hard, masculine lines of his body in every fiber of her being.

"I didn't understand, babe," he said in a hoarse whisper. "I'm sorry."

Sharon couldn't speak, and when Tony turned her and drew her into his arms, she hid her face in the warm strength of his shoulder. He buried his fingers in her hair.

"I made a lot of mistakes," he told her after a long time.

Sharon nodded, lifting her head but unable to meet Tony's eyes. "So did I," she confessed. "I—I think I'd better go."

His embrace tightened for an instant, as though he didn't want to release her, and then relaxed. Sharon collected her purse, hurried out to the garage and slid behind the wheel of her roadster.

The door rolled open at an electronic command from the small control unit she carried in the car, and Sharon backed slowly out into the driveway.

Saying goodbye to Briana and Matt didn't even occur to her.

4

Sharon's small garden apartment seemed to have all the ambience of a jail cell when she walked into it late that afternoon, carrying a bag of take-out food in one hand. The walls were nicotine yellow, unadorned by pictures or any other decoration, and the cheap furniture had served a number of previous tenants.

Feeling overwhelmingly lonely, as she always did when she left the house and the kids to return to this place, Sharon flipped on the television set and sank onto the couch to eat fish-and-chips and watch the shopping channel.

She was teetering on the brink of ordering a set of marble-handled screwdrivers when there was a knock at the door. Sharon turned down the volume, crumpled the evidence of her fast-food dinner into a ball and tossed it into the trash as she called, ''Who's there?''

"It's me," a feminine voice replied. "Helen."

Sharon crossed the short distance between the kitchenette and the front door and admitted her employee with a smile. In her early thirties, like Sharon, Helen was a beautiful woman with sleek black hair and a trim, petite figure. Her almond-shaped eyes accented her Oriental heritage.

Helen's glance fell on Sharon's overnight bag, which was still sitting on the floor in front of the coat closet. "How were the kids?" she asked.

Sharon looked away. "Fine," she answered, as her friend perched gracefully on the arm of an easy chair.

Helen sighed. "You're awfully quiet. What went wrong?"

Sharon pretended not to hear the question. She went into the kitchenette, took two mugs from the cupboard and asked brightly, "Coffee?"

"Sure," Helen replied, and Sharon jumped because she hadn't heard her friend's approach. It seemed that people were always sneaking up on her.

She filled the mugs with water, thrust them into her small microwave oven and set the dial, still avoiding Helen's gaze.

"My, but we're uncommunicative tonight," the younger woman observed. "Did you have some kind of run-in with Tony?"

Sharon swallowed, and her eyes burned for a moment. "Listen," she said in a voice that was too bright and too quick, "I've been thinking that I should do something about this place—you know, paint and get some decent furniture...."

Helen put a hand on Sharon's shoulder. "What happened?" she pressed gently.

Sharon bit into her lower lip and shook her head. "Nothing dramatic," she answered, after a few seconds had passed.

The timer bell on the microwave chimed, and Sharon was grateful for the distraction. She took the cups of steaming water out and transferred them to the counter, where she spooned instant coffee into each one.

Helen sighed and followed Sharon into the living room. "I stopped by to borrow your burgundy shoes," she said. "The ones with the snakeskin toes."

Sharon was looking at the television set. The sound was still off, so the man selling crystal cake plates seemed to be miming his routine. "Help yourself," she replied.

Helen went into Sharon's tiny bedroom and came out a short time later with the shoes in one hand and a firm conviction in her eyes. "Why don't you give it up and go home, Sharon?" she asked quietly. "You know you're not happy without Tony."

"It isn't as simple as that," Sharon confessed.

"Is he involved with someone else?"

Sharon shook her head. "I don't think so. The kids would have mentioned it."

"Well?"

"It's too late, Helen. Too much has happened."

Helen sat on the arm of the chair again, lifted her cup from the end table and took a thoughtful sip of coffee. "I see," she said, looking inscrutable.

Sharon assessed the dingy walls of her living room and said with forced good cheer, "It's time I got on with my life. I'm going to start by turning this place into a home."

"Terrific," agreed Helen, her expression still bland. "If you're going to start embroidering samplers, I'm out of here."

Sharon laughed. "You know, that's not a bad idea. I could do some profound motto in cross-stitch—Anybody Who Says Money Doesn't Buy Happiness Has Never Been to Neiman-Marcus.''

At last, Helen smiled. "Words to live by," she said, setting aside her coffee and standing up. "Well, I've got a hot date with my husband, so I'd better fly. See you tomorrow at the shop." She held up the burgundy pumps as she opened the door. "Thanks for the loan of the shoes," she finished, and then she was gone.

Sharon was even lonelier than before. Knowing that the only cure for that was action, she put on a jacket, gave her hair a quick brushing and fled the apartment for a nearby discount store.

When she returned, she had several gallons of paint and all the attending equipment, except for a ladder. It seemed silly to buy something like that when there were several in the garage at home; she would stop by the house when she left Teddy Bares the next day and pick one up.

Sharon had never painted before, and it took all her forbearance to keep from plunging into the task that very night before any of the preparations had been made.

She rested her hands on her hips as she considered the changes ahead. She'd chosen a pretty shade of ivory for the living room, the palest blue for the kitchenette and a pastel pink for the bedroom and bath. If it killed her, she was going to give this apartment some pizzazz and personality.

While she was at it, she might as well do the same for the rest of her life. It was time to start meeting new men.

Sharon caught one fingernail between her teeth and grimaced. "Exactly how does a person go about doing that?" she asked the empty room.

There was no answer, of course.

Sharon took a shower, washed and blow-dried her hair and got into pajamas. She was settled in bed, reading, when the doorbell rang.

She padded out into the dark living room. "Yes?"

"Mom," Bri wailed from the hallway, "I'm a bastard!"

Sharon wrenched open the door, appalled to find the child standing there, alone, at that late hour. "You aren't, either," she argued practically, as she pulled Briana into the apartment.

"Yes, I am," Bri cried, with all the woe and passion a wounded twelve-year-old is capable of feeling. Her face was dirty and tear streaked, and she hadn't bothered to zip her jacket. "My whole life is ruined! I want to join the Foreign Region!''

''That's 'legion,' darling,'' Sharon said softly, leading her toward a chair, ''and I don't think they take women.''

''More chauvinists.'' Bri sniffled, dashing at her tears with the back of one hand.

''They're everywhere,'' Sharon commiserated, bending to kiss the top of the girl's head. ''Does your dad know where you are?''

''No,'' Bri replied without hesitation, ''and I don't care if he worries, either!''

''Well, I do,'' Sharon answered, reaching for the living room extension and punching out the familiar number. ''I take it you had that talk about your conception,'' she ventured in tones she hoped were diplomatic, as the ringing began at the other end of the line.

Bri was fairly tearing off her jacket, every motion designed to let Sharon know that she was here to stay. The child nodded and sniffled loudly.

Sharon turned away to hide her smile when Tony answered, ''Hello?''

''It's ten o'clock,'' Sharon said warmly. ''Do you know where your daughter is?''

''In bed,'' Tony replied, sounding puzzled.

"Wrong," Sharon retorted. "I'm sorry, Mr. Morelli, but you don't win the week's supply of motor oil and the free trip to Bremerton. Bri is here, and she's very upset."

"How the hell did she manage that?"

Sharon shrugged, even though Tony couldn't see the gesture. "Maybe she called a cab or took a bus—I don't know. The point is—"

"The point is that I hate my father!" Bri shouted, loudly enough for Tony to hear.

He sighed.

"I see everything went very well between the two of you," Sharon chimed sweetly. Her hackles were rising now; she was thinking of the danger Bri had been in and of the pain she was feeling. "Tony, what the devil did you say to this child?"

"He said," Bri began dramatically, "that he and my mother were such animals that they couldn't even wait to be married!"

Sharon turned, one hand over the receiver. "I'd keep quiet, if I were you," she said in warm, dulcet tones. Tony, meanwhile, was quietly swearing on the other end of the line.

"I'll be right over to get her," he announced when he'd finished.

"And leave Matt alone?" Sharon countered. "I don't think so."

"Then you can bring her home."

Sharon was angered by his presumption. "Maybe," she began stiffly, "it would be better if Bri spent the night. She's very upset, and—"

"Briana is my daughter, Sharon," Tony interrupted coldly, "and I'll decide how this is going to be handled."

Sharon felt as though he'd slapped her. *Briana is my daughter.* Tony had never hurled those words in Sharon's face before, never pointed out the fact that, in reality, Bri was exclusively his child.

"I'm sorry," he said into the stricken silence.

She couldn't speak.

"Damn it, Sharon, are you there or not?"

She swallowed. "I-I'll bring Briana home in a few minutes," she said.

"I don't want to go back there ever again!" Bri put in.

Tony's sigh was ragged. Again, he swore. "And I thought I was tactful."

Sharon's eyes were full of tears, and her sinuses had closed. "Apparently not," she said brokenly.

"She can stay," Tony conceded.

Sharon shoved a hand through her hair. "That's magnanimous of you," she replied. "Good night, Tony." Then, not trusting herself to say more, she hung up.

During the next few minutes, while Bri was in the bathroom washing her face and putting on a pair of Sharon's pajamas, her stepmother made the sofa out into a bed. Tony's words were still falling on her soul like drops of acid. *Briana is my daughter...I'll decide how this is going to be handled....*

Bri came out of the bathroom, looking sheepish and very childlike. The emotional storm had evidently blown over. "Is Daddy mad at me?"

Sharon shook her head. "I don't think so, sweetie. But you were plenty mad at him, weren't you?"

Bri nodded, biting her lower lip, and sat down on the end of the sofa bed.

Sharon joined her, putting an arm around the child's shoulders. "Want to talk?"

Bri's chin quivered. "I'm a mistake!" she whispered, and tears were brimming in her eyes again.

Sharon hugged her. "Never."

The little girl sniffled. "I was probably con-

ceived in the back seat of a Chevy or something,'' she despaired.

Sharon couldn't help laughing. ''Oh, Bri,''
she said, pressing her forehead to her stepdaughter's. ''I love you so much.''

Briana flung her arms around Sharon's neck.
''I love you, too, Mom,'' she answered with
weary exuberance. ''I wish you could come
home and stay there.''

Sharon didn't comment on that. Instead, she
smoothed Bri's wildly tangled hair with one
hand and said, ''It's time for you to go to sleep,
but first I want to know something. How did you
get here?''

Bri drew herself up. ''I called a cab. Dad was
doing laundry, so he didn't hear me go out.''

Sharon sighed. ''Sweetheart, what you did
was really dangerous. Do I have your word that
you won't try this ever again?''

Bri hesitated. ''What if I need to talk to you?''

Sharon cupped the lovely face, a replica of
Carmen's, in her hands. ''Then you just call, and
we'll make plans to get together right away,''
she answered softly. ''Do you promise, Briana?''

The child swallowed hard and nodded, and
then Sharon tucked her into bed and kissed her

good-night just as she had so many times in the
past. She'd reached the privacy of her room before her heart cracked into two pieces and the
grieving began in earnest.

Tony arrived early the next morning while
Sharon was still in the shower, and collected Briana. He left a terse note on the kitchen table,
thanking her for "everything."

Sharon crumpled the note and flung it at the
wall. "Thank you for everything, too, Morelli,"
she muttered. "Thanks one hell of a lot!"

She was in a terrible mood by the time she
reached the shop. Helen had already arrived, and
Teddy Bares was open for business.

Since there were several customers browsing,
Sharon made herself smile as she stormed behind the counter and into the small office at the
back.

Helen appeared in the doorway after a few
minutes had passed. "Are you okay?" she ventured carefully.

"No," Sharon replied.

"Is there anything I can do?"

Sharon shook her head. She was going to have
to pull herself together and get on with the day.
It was a sure bet that Tony wasn't standing
around agonizing over the fact that his family

was in pieces. He knew how to set aside his personal life when it was time to concentrate on work.

Sharon drew a deep breath and went out to greet her customers. The morning was a busy one, fortunately, and there wasn't time to think about anything but taking care of business.

It was noon, and Helen had gone to the pizza place at the other end of the mall to get take-out salads, when Tony wandered in. Instead of his usual jeans, work shirt and boots, he was wearing a three-piece suit, beautifully tailored to his build. He approached the counter and inclined his head slightly to one side, his dark eyes seeming to caress Sharon for a moment before he spoke.

"I'm sorry we didn't get a chance to talk this morning," he said.

"I'll bet you are," Sharon scoffed, remembering the brisk note tucked between the salt-and-pepper shakers in the middle of her table. "What's with the fancy clothes?"

"I had a meeting," Tony answered. Then he arched one ebony eyebrow and sighed. "I don't suppose you're free for lunch."

Sharon opened her mouth to say that he was dead right, but Helen arrived before she could get the words out. "Know what?" she chimed. "They were all out of salad. I guess you have no choice but to accept Tony's invitation."

Sharon wasn't buying the no-salad routine—the pizza place made the stuff up by the bushel—and she frowned at Helen, wondering where she'd hidden all that lettuce. "I've got an idea," she told her friend tartly. "Why don't you go to lunch with Tony?"

Like a spectator at a tennis match, Tony turned his head toward Helen, waiting for her to return the ball.

"I have plans," Helen said loftily, and marched around behind the counter, elbowing Sharon aside. "It just so happens that I'm out to build an underwear empire of my own, Ms. Morelli, so watch your back."

Tony laughed and took Sharon's arm and, rather than make a scene, she allowed him to lead her out of the shop and along the mall's crowded concourse. The place was jammed with mothers and children shopping for school clothes.

Sharon jutted out her chin and walked a little faster, ignoring Tony as best she could.

"Where do you want to eat?" he finally asked.

"I don't care," Sharon responded firmly.

"I like a decisive woman," came the taut reply. Tony's grasp on her elbow tightened, and he propelled her toward a sandwich place filled with brass and hanging plants.

When they were seated at a table in a corner by a window, Sharon's rigid control began to falter a little. "How could you say that?" she demanded in a miserable whisper, avoiding Tony's eyes.

"What?" he asked, in a baffled tone that made Sharon want to clout him over the head with the menu that had just been shoved into her hands.

"What you said last night," Sharon whispered furiously. "About Bri being your daughter!"

"Isn't she?" Tony asked, having the audacity to read the menu while he awaited her answer.

Sharon suppressed an urge to kick him in the shin. She pushed back her chair and would have left the table if he hadn't reached out and caught hold of one of her wrists. "You know that isn't what I mean!" she said.

Tony looked as though he had a headache. *Men,* Sharon thought to herself, *are such babies when it comes to pain.* "We do not seem to be communicating, here,'' he observed a few moments later.

"That's because one of us is stupid,'' Sharon said. "And it isn't me, buddy.''

Tony sighed. "Maybe I was a little insensitive—''

"A little?'' Sharon drew a deep breath and let it out. "My God, Tony, you've got insensitivity down to an art. You don't even know why I'm angry!''

His jaw tightened. "I'm sure after you've tortured me for a few hours,'' he responded, "you'll tell me!''

A teenage waitress stepped into the breach. "The special today is baked chicken.''

"We'll take it,'' said Tony, his dark, furious gaze never shifting from Sharon's face.

"Right,'' said the waitress with a shrug, swinging her hips as she walked away.

Tony didn't wait for Sharon to speak. "So help me God,'' he told her in an ominously low voice, "if you say you don't want the baked chicken, I'll strangle you.''

Sharon sniffed. "I had no idea you felt so strongly about poultry,'' she said.

Tony glared at her. "Sharon,'' he warned.

She sat back. "Bri is not just your daughter,

regardless whose Chevy she was conceived in,'' she said with dignity. ''I raised that child. I love her as much as I love Matthew.''

Tony looked bewildered. ''Regardless of whose...'' His words fell away as an expression of furious revelation dawned in his face. ''Last night. You're still mad because of what I said last night on the phone about Bri being my daughter.''

Sharon said nothing; she didn't need to, because she knew the look on her face said it all.

''Good Lord,'' Tony muttered. ''I apologized for that.''

Sharon was dangerously near tears; she willed herself not to cry. She had a store in this mall; people knew her. She couldn't afford to make a public spectacle of herself. ''And you thought that made everything all right, didn't you? You could just say 'I'm sorry' and it would be as though it had never happened.''

The baked chicken arrived. When the waitress had gone, Tony demanded, ''What else could I have said, Sharon?''

She swallowed and looked down at her food in real despair. Never in a million years was she going to be able to get so much as a bite down her throat. ''Bri is mine, too, and I love her,'' she insisted miserably, and then she got up and walked out of the restaurant with her head held high.

The shop was full of customers when Sharon got back, and she threw herself into waiting on them. All the same, it was a relief when the day ended. Unlike many other shops in the mall, Teddy Bares closed at five-thirty.

"You really ought to think about getting someone in to work until nine," Helen ventured quietly as the two women went through the familiar routine of emptying the cash register, totaling receipts and locking up.

Sharon just shrugged. She felt raw inside and had ever since her encounter with Tony at noon. Going through the motions was the best she could hope to accomplish, for the moment, anyway.

Helen's gaze was sympathetic. "What happened, Sharon?" she asked. At her friend's look, she went on. "I know, it's none of my business, but I've never seen two people more in love than you and Tony. And yet here you are, divorced—unable to have a civilized lunch together."

Sharon remained stubbornly silent, hoping that Helen would let the subject drop.

She wasn't about to be so accommodating.

"He loves you, Sharon," she said insistently. "The rest of us see that so clearly—why can't you?"

The numbers on the receipts blurred together. Sharon chose to ignore Helen's remark about Tony's feelings. "You know, my mother warned me that the marriage wouldn't work. Tony was already successful then, and Bea said he was way out of my league—that he'd get tired of me and start running around."

Helen was seething; Sharon didn't even have to look at her friend to know that smoke was practically blowing out of her ears. "Excuse my bluntness, but what the devil does your mother know? Who is she, Dr. Ruth?" Helen paused. "Tony didn't cheat on you, did he?"

Sharon shook her head. "No, but he got tired of me. I'm sure it would only have been a matter of time until there were other women."

Helen made a sound that resembled a suppressed scream. "How do you know he got tired of you? Did he say so?"

"No," Sharon answered in a sad, reflective tone. "He didn't have to. He worked more and more, harder and harder, and when we were together, we fought—like today."

"What did you fight about?" Helen persisted.

Sharon looked around her at the teddies and peignoirs and robes, all made from shimmering silks and satins of the highest quality. "Teddy Bares, mostly," she answered. And then she took up her purse and started toward the door.

The subject, like the shop, was closed.

5

Tony slammed his fist on the hood of a pickup truck marked with the company name, and swore. He'd just fired one of the best foremen in the construction business, and now he was going to have to swallow his pride, go after the man and apologize.

"Tony."

He stiffened at the sound of his father's voice, then turned, reluctantly, to face him. "You heard," he said.

Vincent Morelli was a man of medium height and build, and of quiet dignity. He'd begun his working life as an apprentice carpenter at fifteen and had passed a thriving company on to his sons fifty years later. "Everybody heard," he replied. "What happened, Tonio?"

Tony shoved one hand through his hair. "I'm not sure, Papa," he confessed, shifting his gaze to the line of condominiums under construction a hundred yards away. "I know one thing—I was wrong. I've been wrong a lot lately."

Vincent came to stand beside him, bracing one booted foot against the front bumper of the truck. "I'm listening," he said.

Tony had heard those words often from both his parents since earliest childhood, and he knew Vincent meant them. He was grateful for the solid, sensible upbringing he'd had, and he wanted desperately to give the same gift to his own children. "It's Sharon," he said. "And the kids—it's everything."

Vincent waited, saying nothing.

"I didn't want the divorce," Tony went on after a few moments, aware that he wasn't telling his father anything he didn't already know. Vincent had seen the grief and pain Tony had hidden so carefully from Sharon. "Ever since it happened, I've been trying to find a way to make things right again. Papa, I can't even talk to the woman without making her mad as hell."

His father smiled sadly. He'd always liked Sharon, even defended her desire to strike out on her own. Vincent had insisted that she was only trying to prove herself by starting the shop, while Tony had dismissed the project as silly. And worse.

"In some ways, Tonio," Vincent said, his voice quiet and calm, "you're too much like me."

Tony was taken aback; there was no one he admired more than his father. It was impossible to be too much like him.

"I worked hard building this company for many, many years. But I was also something of a failure as a man and as a father. I didn't know my own sons until they were men, working beside me, and I may never truly know my daughters."

Tony started to protest, but Vincent stopped him with one upraised hand, still callused from years of labor, and went on. "You all grew up to be successful men, you and Michael and Richard, and your sisters are fine women, but you give me too much of the credit. Most of it should go to your mother, Tony, because she taught you all the things that make you strong—confidence in yourself, clear thinking, personal responsibility, integrity."

Tony looked down at his boots.

"I was sixty years old," Vincent continued, "before I had the good sense to appreciate Maria for the woman she is. If you're wise, Tonio, you won't wait that long before you start treating Sharon with the respect she deserves.''

"I do respect her," Tony said, his eyes still downcast. "She came into my life at a time when I thought I wanted to die, Papa, and she gave me back my soul. And even though she'd had a rotten childhood herself, she knew how to be a mother to Bri.''

Vincent laid a hand on his son's shoulder. "These are pretty words, Tony. Perhaps if you would say them to Sharon, instead of assuming that she knows how you feel, things might get better.''

"She won't listen. There are always too many demands—too many distractions—''

"That is simple to fix," Vincent broke in reasonably. "You bring the children to your mother and me and you persuade Sharon to go to the island house for a couple of days. There, you hold her hand and you speak softly, always. You make sure that there is wine and music, and you tell her that you love her. Often.''

Tony grinned, feeling a certain tentative hope. "You're quite the ladies' man, Papa," he teased.

Vincent chuckled and slapped his son's shoulder again. "I did not father three sons and three daughters by accident," he replied.

Just then, the recently fired foreman drove up in a swirl of dust. Scrambling out of his car, the man stormed toward Tony, shaking his finger. "I've got a few more things to say to you, Morelli!" he bellowed.

Tony sighed, gave his father a sheepish look and went to meet his angry ex-employee. "I've got something to say to you, too," he responded evenly. "I was wrong, Charlie, and I'm sorry."

Charlie Petersen stared at him in astonishment. "Say what?" he finally drawled.

"You heard me," Tony said. "There's a foreman's job open if you want it."

Charlie grinned. "I want it," he admitted.

The two men shook hands, and then Charlie strode back toward the framework rising against the sky. "Hey, Merkins," he called out to a member of his crew. "If I see you walking around without your hard hat again, you're out of here, union steward or not!"

Tony laughed and went back to his own work.

Sharon had left the shop early in hopes of getting the stepladder from the garage without encountering Tony. Conversely, she was almost disappointed that she'd succeeded.

"I wish we could come and help you," Matt

said, as they gathered in the kitchen to say good-bye, biting forlornly into a cookie, "but we're both grounded."

Bri, perched on one of the stools at the breakfast bar, nodded disconsolately.

Sharon pretended to ponder their offenses, a finger to her chin. "Let's see," she said to Matt, "you're being punished for the wholesale slaughter of goldfish, am I right?"

Matt gave Bri an accusing look, but admitted his guilt with a nod.

"And I'm on the list," Briana supplied glumly, "because Dad says running away isn't cool."

"He's right," Sharon said. "Did the two of you manage to work things out?"

Bri shook her head. "Not yet. We're supposed to talk tonight."

Sharon sighed and laid gentle hands on her stepdaughter's shoulders. "Sometimes your dad isn't the most tactful man on earth. You might try looking past what he says to what he means."

"You could try that, too, Mom," Bri remarked, with the kind of out-of-left-field astuteness children sometimes use to put their elders in their places.

"Touché," Sharon replied, kissing Bri's forehead and then Matt's.

Matt groaned, but spared her his usual, heartfelt "yuck!" "How are we supposed to get Uncle Michael a birthday present if we're both grounded?" he demanded, when Sharon would have made her exit.

"Gramma already told us the party will have to be postponed because Uncle Michael is going to be out of town and because Daddy has other plans for the weekend," Bri told him in a tone reserved for little brothers and other lower forms of life. "Boy, are you stupid."

Sharon closed her eyes. She didn't want to give a damn that Tony had a special date lined up for the weekend, but she did. Oh, hell, did she ever.

Matt wasn't about to stand for any nonsense from his sister. "Saturday is still Uncle Michael's birthday and we still have to get him a present and you're *still* a royal pain in the rear end, Briana Morelli!"

Reminding herself that the job of worrying about these two little darlings was rightfully Tony's—bless his heart—Sharon backed out of the door, waving. "Bye," she chimed, as the argument escalated into a confrontation that might well require peacekeeping forces.

Mrs. Harry, the housekeeper, would keep them from killing each other before Tony got home.

The stepladder was leaning against the wall of the garage, where Sharon had left it. She put it into the trunk of the roadster along with her oldest pair of jeans from the dresser upstairs and two ancient work ~~shirts~~ that she'd stolen from Tony's side of the closet.

The refurbishing of Sharon Morelli and her surroundings was about to begin.

Two and a half hours later, when Sharon had moved and covered all her furniture and masked off every inch of baseboard, every electrical outlet and every window in her apartment, she was starting to wish she'd been more resistant to change, more of a stick-in-the-mud.

There was a resolute knock at the door—her dinner was about to be delivered, no doubt—and Sharon unwrapped the knob and turned it. Tony was standing in the hallway, paying the kid from the Chinese restaurant. He'd already appropriated her pork-fried rice and sweet-and-sour chicken.

Sharon snatched the white cartons from her

ex-husband's possession and went into the kitchen to untape one of the drawers and get out a spoon and fork.

"Oh, are you still here?" she asked pleasantly, when she turned to find Tony standing behind her with his arms folded and his damnably handsome head cocked to one side.

"No," he answered dryly, his eyes smiling at her in a way that melted her pelvic bones. "I'm only an illusion. It's all done with mirrors."

"I wish," Sharon muttered, edging around him to march back into the living room, her feet making a crackling sound on the newspaper covering the carpet. She knew she looked something less than glamorous, wearing a bandana over her hair, those disreputable jeans, dirty sneakers and a shirt that reached to her knees, but one couldn't paint walls and ceilings in a flowing caftan.

Tony followed her. He was too big for her apartment; he didn't fit.

Sharon wished that he'd leave and at the very same moment was glad he hadn't. "Sit down," she said with a generous gesture. Then, realizing that both chairs were covered, along with the couch, she plunked down on the floor, Indian-fashion.

Tony joined her, solemnly raising his right hand. "How, please pass the peace pipe and all that other Native American stuff," he said.

Sharon smiled, opened her food and began to eat. "I'd offer you some," she said through a mouthful of fried rice, "but I'm incredibly greedy."

Tony's eyes left Sharon warm wherever they touched her, which was everywhere, and he let her remark hang unanswered in the air.

She squirmed and speared a chunk of sauce-covered chicken from the carton on the floor in front of her. "Are you here for some specific reason or what?" she asked.

He looked around at all the masking and newspapering she'd done. "I came to help you paint," he said.

Sharon sighed. "Tony—"

He was watching her mouth. Sharon found it very distracting when he did that. "Yes?" The word had a low rumble, like a faraway earthquake.

"I can manage this on my own."

His smile was a little forced, but it was a smile. He was trying; Sharon had to give him credit for that. "I'm sure you can," he answered reasonably. "But I'd like to help." He spread his hands. "Call it a personal quirk."

"I call it a crock," Sharon responded, but she was grinning. She couldn't help herself.

"I love you," Tony said quietly.

Sharon's forkful of fried rice hung suspended between the carton and her mouth. She remembered what the kids had said about the plans he'd made and stiffened her spine. "Are you practicing for your hot date this weekend?" she asked.

"Jealous?" he wanted to know.

"Not in the least," lied Sharon, jamming the fork into her rice as if it were a climber's flag she was planting on a mountain peak.

Tony reached out, took the carton from her hand and set it aside. Then he caught her wrists gently in his hands and pulled until she was straddling his lap. "Just this once," he suggested, breathing the words rather than saying them, his lips brushing against Sharon's, "let's skip the preliminary rounds, okay?"

Sharon's arms were trembling as she draped them around his neck. "Okay," she whispered. She knew that what was about to happen was a mistake, but she couldn't stop it. Tony was a man any woman would want, and Sharon had the added handicap of loving him.

The kiss was long and thorough and so intimate that it left Sharon disoriented. She was surprised to find herself lying on the floor, because she didn't remember moving. And she was frightened by the scope of her feelings.

Tony's hand was unfastening the buttons on her shirt when she stopped him by closing her fingers over his. "This woman you're seeing this weekend—who is she?" she dared to ask.

He kissed her again, briefly this time, and playfully. "She's you," he answered. "If you don't turn me down, that is."

Sharon withdrew her hand, and the unbuttoning continued, unimpeded. She closed her eyes as he opened the shirt and then removed it. She made a soft sound in her throat when she felt the front catch on her bra give way. "Oh, Tony—"

"Is that a yes or a no?" he asked in a husky voice, and Sharon could feel his breath fanning over her nipple.

"What's the...question?" she countered, gasping and arching her back slightly when she felt the tip of Tony's tongue touch her.

He chuckled and took several moments to enjoy the territory he'd just marked as his own before answering, ''We'll talk about it later.''

Sharon's fingers had buried themselves, at no conscious order from her, in his hair. She felt an inexplicable happiness founded on nothing of substance. Her eyes were burning, and there was an achy thickness in her throat.

His hand was warm as it cupped her breast, his thumb shaping a nipple still moist and taut from the caresses of his lips and tongue. ''Oh, God, I've missed you,'' he said, and then he kissed her again, hungrily, as though to consume her.

And she wanted to be consumed.

Tony's mouth strayed downward, along the line of her arched neck, over her bare shoulder, midway down her upper arm. When he reclaimed her nipple, Sharon moaned an anguished welcome.

The snap on her jeans gave way to his fingers, closely followed by the zipper, and still he availed himself of her breasts, first one and then the other. Sharon was like a woman in the throes of an uncontrollable fever; she flung her head from side to side, blinded by the sensations Tony was creating with his hand and mouth, her breath too shallow and too quick. She grasped his T-shirt in her hands and pulled at it; if she'd had the strength, she would have torn it from him.

He finally cooperated, however, allowing Sharon to undress him, to pleasure him in some of the same ways that he had pleasured her.

Their joining, when it happened, was graceful at first, like a ballet. With each flexing of their bodies it became more frenzied, though, culminating in a kind of sweet desperation, a tangling of triumph and surrender that left both Tony and Sharon exhausted.

Tony recovered first and, after giving Sharon a leisurely kiss, sat up and began putting his clothes back on. The newspaper crackled as he moved, and Sharon began to laugh.

"What's funny?" he asked, turning and bracing himself with his hands so that he was poised over her. His eyes were full of love and mischief.

"I probably have newsprint on my backside," Sharon replied.

"Turn over and I'll look," Tony offered generously.

"Thanks, but no thanks," she answered, sliding out from beneath him and reaching for her own clothes.

"'Housing Market Bottoms Out,'" he pretended to read in a ponderous tone when Sharon reached for her panties and jeans.

She laughed and swung at him with the jeans, and that started a bout of wrestling, which ended in Sharon's bed a long time later.

"What were you going to ask me—about the weekend?" Sharon ventured, her cheek resting against Tony's shoulder. It felt good to lie close to him like that again.

Tony rested his chin on top of her head. He seemed to be bracing himself for a rebuff of some sort. "I'd like to go to the island house for a couple of days—just you and me."

Sharon absorbed that in silence. She had planned to take inventory at the shop that weekend, but a woman in business has to be flexible. She sighed contentedly and kissed the bare skin of his shoulder. "Sounds like an indecent proposal to me."

He laughed and his arm tightened around her waist. "Believe me, lady, it is."

Sharon raised her head to squint at the clock on the bedside table. "Oh, Lord. Tony, who's with the kids?"

"Mrs. Harry stayed late. Why? What time is it?"

"Boy, did Mrs. Harry stay late," Sharon agreed. "Tony, it's after midnight."

He swore and threw back the covers, crunching around on the newspaper looking for his clothes, and Sharon laughed.

"Do you realize what that woman gets for overtime?" Tony demanded, bringing his jeans and T-shirt from the living room to put them on.

Sharon was still giggling. "No, but I know how much she hates working late. I'm glad you're the one who has to face Scary Harry, and not me."

"Thanks a lot," Tony replied, snatching his watch from the bedside table. "We're leaving for the island Friday night," he warned, bending over to kiss her once more, "so make sure you have all the bases covered."

Sharon opened her mouth to protest this arbitrary treatment, then closed it again. She really didn't want to argue, and they could discuss such issues on the island.

"Good night, babe," Tony said from the doorway of her room.

Sharon felt a sudden and infinite sadness because he was leaving. "Bye," she replied, glad that he couldn't see her face.

After she'd heard the door close behind him,

she went out to put the chain lock in place. This, she thought, was what it was like to have a lover instead of a husband.

She tried to decide which she preferred while picking up her clothes. Lovers had a way of disappearing, like smoke, but husbands were surely more demanding. Sharon guessed that this was a case of six in one hand and half a dozen in the other.

She also deduced pretty quickly that she wasn't going to be able to crawl back into that bed where she'd just spent hours making love with Tony and fall placidly to sleep. She took a shower, put on her clothes and mixed the first batch of paint.

The new coat of soft ivory revitalized the living room and, coupled with the after effects of Tony's lovemaking, it brightened Sharon's spirits, as well. For the first time in months—the first time since she'd filed for divorce—she felt real hope for the future.

It was 3:00 a.m. when she finished. After cleaning up the mess, Sharon stumbled off to her room and collapsed facedown on the rumpled covers of the bed. She had absolutely no problem sleeping.

She entered Teddy Bares, bright eyed and

humming, at precisely nine o'clock the next morning to find Helen reading a romance novel behind the counter.

The cover showed a dashing pirate holding a lushly buxom beauty in his arms. There were eager lights in Helen's eyes as she told Sharon breathlessly, "The woman in this book was given the choice of sleeping in the hold with a lot of soiled doves on their way to Morocco or sharing the captain's bed!"

Sharon took the book and studied the hero on the cover. He was an appealing rake with a terrific body. "Share his bed or languish in the hold, huh? Decisions, decisions."

Helen reclaimed the paperback and put it under the counter with her purse. Her expression was watchful now, and curious. "You look happy," she said suspiciously.

Sharon took her own purse to the back room and dropped it into a drawer of her desk. After settling herself in her chair, she reached for a pad of legal paper and a pencil and began making notes for an ad in the help wanted column of the newspaper. "Thank you," she replied in belated response to Helen's remark. "We won't be taking inventory this weekend, but I'll need you to work on Saturday if you will."

Helen was reading over her shoulder. "You're hiring another clerk? Excuse me, but is there something I should know?"

Sharon stopped writing and smiled up at her friend. "Good heavens, are you asking me if I mean to fire you?"

Helen nodded. "I guess I am," she said, looking worried.

Sharon shook her head. "Absolutely not. But I've decided that you're right—it's time we got someone to work evenings, and I'd like to be able to take more time off. That means we need two people, really. Both part-time."

Out front, the counter bell rang. Helen was forced to go and wait on a customer, but she returned as soon as she could. Sharon was on the telephone by that time, placing her ad.

"With any luck, we'll have applicants by Monday," she said, hanging up.

Helen's eyes were wide. "I know what's going on here!" she cried in triumph. "It's like that Jimmy Stewart movie where he wishes he'd never been born and *whammie*, this angel fixes him right up. His friends don't recognize him— his own mother doesn't recognize him. His whole life is changed because he realizes how important he really is, and he's so happy—"

Sharon was shaking her head and smiling indulgently. "You can't seriously think that anything like that really happened," she said. "Can you?"

Helen sighed and shook her head. "No, but sometimes I get carried away."

With a nod, Sharon got out the books and began tallying debits and credits.

6

"The pictures have to go, Mama," Tony said gently, gesturing toward the photographs of Carmen and himself on top of his parents' television set.

Maria Morelli looked down at her hands, which were folded in her lap. She was a beautiful woman who always wore her dark hair done up in an impeccable coronet, and her skin was as smooth as Italian porcelain. Although she was the finest cook in all the family, her figure was trim, like those of her daughters. "Carmen's mother was my dearest friend," she finally replied, her voice small and soft. "We might as well have been sisters."

Tony nodded. "I know that, Mama. I'm just trying to make things a little easier for Sharon, that's all."

The flawless, ageless face hardened for the merest fraction of a second. "Sharon divorced you,'' she reminded him. ''She is not your wife.''

Tony let out the sigh he had been restraining. ''Do you dislike her that much, Mama?'' he asked quietly, after a few moments had passed.

''I don't dislike Sharon at all,'' Maria replied, her dark eyes snapping as she met her eldest son's gaze. ''She is my grandson's mother.'' She paused, probably to allow Tony time to absorb the significance of such a bond.

''The pictures bother her,'' Tony reasoned. ''You can understand that, can't you?''

''Carmen was practically family. You were raised together from the time you were babies—''

''Yes,'' Tony interjected softly. ''And I loved Carmen very much. But she's dead now—''

''All the more reason she should be remembered properly,'' Maria said, and although her voice was low, it was also passionate. ''Have you forgotten that she was Briana's mother, Tonio?''

Tony shook his head. ''No, Mama. But Sharon isn't asking any of us to forget.''

Maria drew in a long breath, let it out slowly and nodded. Her glance strayed to the assortment of pictures she'd kept for twelve years, lingering fondly on each one in turn. "She was so beautiful, Tonio."

Tony looked at Carmen, smiling happily and holding his arm in their wedding picture, and some of the old feelings came back, if only for a moment. "Yes," he said hoarsely.

"You take the pictures," Maria said, with an abrupt sweep of her hand that didn't fool Tony in the least. "Save them for Briana—someday, she'll want them."

Tony nodded and rose to stack the framed photographs one on top of the other. Maria had left her chair to stand with her back to him. "You still love Sharon, then?" she asked.

"Yes," Tony replied. "Maybe more than before, Mama."

"There were so many problems."

He thought of the hours he'd spent with Sharon during the night just past. Although the sex had been better than ever—and it had always been good, even at the end of their marriage—it was the laughter and the quiet talk that Tony loved to remember. He cherished the images that lingered in his mind. "There isn't anything I want more in all this world than a second chance with Sharon," he told his mother, and then he left the huge house, where every item in every room was familiar.

Tony went to his condo, rather than the house, partly because he needed some time alone and partly because he wanted to give the photographs to Briana at a time when things were better between them. At the moment, his relationship with his daughter was rocky, to say the least.

When he reached the one-bedroom place where he'd been living since the final separation from Sharon, Tony set the photographs of Carmen down and immediately forgot about them. His grandmother, Lucia, made one of her surprise entrances, coming out of the kitchen with her arms extended.

Lucia went wherever she wanted, that being a privilege of age and rank in the Morelli family, and Tony kissed her forehead and greeted her in gentle Italian.

She responded by explaining that his sister, Rosa, had brought her—she knew, as did everyone in the family, where he kept a spare key hidden—and that she wanted to cook for him. Tony adored the old woman, but he wasn't in the mood to eat or to chat amiably.

"Another time," he told Lucia, in her own language. "I can't stay."

Lucia smiled, touched his face with one of her small, veined hands and replied that she would put the food in plastic containers and tuck it into the refrigerator for him to have later.

Tony laughed and shook his head, then bent to kiss her cheek. "Enjoy, Grandmama," he told her, and then he left the condo, got back into his car and drove until he reached the secret place overlooking the sound.

This bit of ground with a view of trees and water was a place to think, a place to hope and hurt and plan. Twice, it had been a place to cry.

Sharon returned from her lunch break with her book tucked away in her purse so that Helen wouldn't see it. What was happening between her and Tony was still too fragile and tentative to discuss, even with her closest friend, and she knew that an Italian cookbook would raise questions.

While Helen was out having her customary salad, Sharon called Tony's sister, Rosa, and enlisted her help. Married two years and pregnant with her first child, Rose was a willing collaborator. She promised to pick up the kids and take them home with her for the evening.

When it came time to close the shop, Sharon rushed through her part of the routine and dashed to the grocery store at the opposite end of the mall. Holding the book two inches from the end of her nose, she studied the list of ingredients needed to make clam spaghetti as she wheeled her cart up and down the aisles. If this dish didn't impress Tony, nothing would.

After leaving the supermarket, Sharon drove to the house on Tamarack Drive and let herself in. In the kitchen, on the big blackboard near the telephone, Bri had written carefully, "Dear Daddy, we're at Aunt Rose's. I told her we were grounded and she said our sentence had been suspended and you're supposed to go to the condo. Love, Bri."

Beneath this Rose had added a scrawled, "Don't worry about Grandmama—I'm on my way to collect her right now. Ciao, handsome. R."

Smiling, Sharon went to the rack where assorted keys were kept and ran her finger along it until she came to the one that would admit her to Tony's place. She dropped it into the pocket of her corduroy skirt and left the house again.

Tony's building stood on a road well out of town; Sharon remembered exactly where it was because he'd been working there overseeing the construction of the place when she'd had him served with divorce papers. The address was burned into her mind, as was the image of Tony storming into Teddy Bares with the papers in his hand, demanding answers Sharon hadn't been able to give.

He lived at the far end of the first row of condos; Bri and Matt had told her that weeks before, after a visit. Sharon pulled into the empty driveway and then sat for several minutes, trying to work up the courage to go in.

Finally, she did, her hand trembling a little as she unlocked the door and stepped inside, her bag of groceries in one arm.

The place was dim and sparsely furnished in the way that homes of divorced men often are, and it was neat to a fault.

A lighted aquarium bubbled on one end of the raised hearth of the fireplace, boasting several brightly colored fish. On the mantel was a framed picture of the kids taken at Disneyland during happier times. Tony's mother, sisters and aunts had supplied him with hand-crocheted pillow covers and afghans, which were discreetly displayed. Sharon knew Tony kept them not because he loved the handiwork, but because he loved the family.

She felt a bittersweet mixture of hope and grief as she switched on a lamp and found her way into the kitchen. Just as she'd expected, it was small and efficient, organized down to the last olive pick. A delicious aroma of tomato sauce and mingling spices filled the air.

Humming, Sharon took the new cookbook from her purse and the groceries from their paper bag. She knew a few moments of chagrin when the telephone rang and Tony's answering machine picked up the call; maybe she shouldn't have let herself in this way without his knowing.

The caller was Tony's youngest brother, Michael. "Get back to me when you can, Tonio," he said with quiet affection. "We landed the contract on that new supermarket, so it's party-time at my place tonight. Bring the blonde."

Sharon's hands froze as Michael's closing words echoed through the condo like something shouted into a cave. She considered gathering up her cookbook and food and leaving, then drew a deep breath and reminded herself that she and Tony were divorced. Certainly, he had a right to date.

On the other hand, it hurt so very much to think of him with someone else....

In the end, Sharon decided to stay. Since she'd come this far, she might as well see this idea through to the last chopped clam and strand of spaghetti.

Sharon soon discovered that she'd forgotten to buy olive oil, and Tony's supply, if he'd ever had one, was gone. "What blonde?" his ex-wife muttered, still a little nettled, as she got down the butter-flavored shortening and plopped some into a skillet.

When she had the meal well underway—she had to admit that it didn't smell like anything Maria Morelli had ever cooked—she decided to switch on some music, touch up her lipstick and make sure that her hair was combed.

The bathroom had to be at the end of the hall next to the front door. Sharon headed that way, but was halted by an eerie glow coming from the single bedroom.

Puzzled, she paused and looked inside, and what she saw made her mouth drop open. The shock wounded her so deeply that she had to grasp the doorjamb in one hand for a moment to steady herself, and just as she found the strength to turn away, she heard Tony coming in.

Still, she stared at the familiar photographs, the ones that had once graced Maria's living room. They were neatly aligned on Tony's dresser, a votive candle flickering in front of them.

Sharon turned away with one hand to her mouth, her eyes scalded with tears, and came up hard against Tony's chest.

He took her upper arms in his hands to steady her, and even though the light was dim in the hallway, Sharon could see the baffled look in his eyes. She broke free of him and stumbled back to the living room, where she grabbed for her purse.

"Sharon, wait a minute," Tony pleaded reasonably. "Don't go—"

She dashed at her tears with the back of one hand and marched into the kitchen to turn off the burner under her clam sauce. "I guess I deserved this," she called, knowing that she probably sounded distracted and hysterical but unable to help herself. When she reached the living room again, Tony was beside the front door, as if to stand guard. "It was presumptuous of me to just walk in, thinking we could pick up where we left off—''

''You're welcome here anytime,'' Tony hold her. ''Day or night.''

''The woman Michael refers to as 'the blonde' would probably take issue with that,'' Sharon said, and the words, intended to be sophisticated and flippant, came out sounding like a pathetic joke. She reached for the doorknob and turned it. ''Goodbye, Tony. And I'm sorry for intruding—I really am.''

When she opened the door, he caught hold of her arm and pulled her back inside. The stereo was playing a particularly romantic tune, one she and Tony had once liked to listen to together.

''Damn it, Sharon, I'm not going to let you walk out. Not again.''

She wrenched her arm free of his grasp. ''You can't stop me,'' she spat, and this time there was no attempt at sounding anything but angry and hurt. She stood with her back to him, trembling, gazing out at the street and seeing nothing.

''You're too upset to drive,'' Tony reasoned, making no attempt to renew his hold on her arm. ''Come in and talk to me. Please.''

Sharon lifted one hand to her forehead for a

moment. "There's no point in our talking—we should have learned that by now."

He sighed. "Sharon, if it's about the woman, we're divorced—"

"It isn't that," she said in wooden tones. "It's that spooky little shrine in your room." She paused on the doorstep, turning to look up at him. "My attorney will be contacting yours about the joint custody arrangement—our sharing the house and all that. We're going to have to work out some other way."

"Sharon." Tony's voice had taken on a note of hoarse desperation. He reached out cautiously to take her hand, and then he pulled her behind him along the hallway toward his room.

In the doorway, he paused. Sharon saw the muscles in his broad shoulders go rigid beneath the fabric of his shirt. "Oh, my God," he muttered, and didn't even turn around to face her. After giving a raspy sigh, he said, "You'll never believe me, so I'm not even going to try to explain. Not right now." His hand released Sharon's, and hers fell back to her side. "I'll call you later."

"There isn't going to be a 'later,'" Sharon said mildly. "Not for us."

With that, she turned and walked away, and Tony made no move to stop her.

Back at the apartment, she changed into work clothes and began painting with a vengeance. Tears streamed down her face as she worked, but she dared not stand still. She painted the kitchen, the bedroom and the bathroom, and gave the living room a second coat.

When that was done it was so late that there was no sense in going to bed at all. Sharon disposed of all the newspaper, leftover paint, brushes and cans, and then took a shower. As she turned around under the spray of water, she scoured her breasts and hips, all the places where Tony had touched her, hoping to wash away the sensations that still lingered.

"My God," Helen breathed, when she walked into the shop an hour later, "you look terrible!"

Sharon said nothing. She simply marched into the back room like a marionette on strings that were too tautly drawn, and sat down at her desk. She got out the checkbook and made out Helen's paycheck, as well as one for herself.

After that, she scanned the morning's mail, taking special note of a fashion show coming up in Paris in a couple of weeks. Maybe it was time to go on a real buying trip instead of ordering everything from wholesalers. She wondered numbly whether or not her passport had expired.

She felt almost ready to go out into the main part of the shop and face the customers by that time, but as Sharon slid back her chair, she got a surprise.

Michael, Tony's brother, came striding into the little room, looking very earnest, very young and very angry. Sharon had always liked him tremendously, and she was injured by the heat she saw burning in his dark Morelli eyes.

"What did you do to him?" he whispered tightly.

"Shall I call the police?" Helen put in from the doorway.

Sharon shook her head and gestured for Helen to leave her alone with Michael. "Sit down," she told her former brother-in-law.

He took the chair beside her desk, still fuming. "I had a party last night," he said, glaring at her.

Sharon sat down and folded her hands in her lap. "I know," she replied evenly.

"Tony was there."

By this time, there was a wall of ice around Sharon. "Good," she answered.

Michael was obviously furious. To his credit,

however, he drew a deep breath and tried to speak reasonably. "Sharon, my brother looks like he's been in a train wreck. He showed up at my place late last night, stinking drunk and carrying on about shrines and blondes and clam sauce. The only halfway reasonable statement I could get out of him was that your lawyer was going to call his lawyer." Michael was a little calmer now. "Which brings us back to my original question. What did you do to Tony?"

Sharon was too tired and too broken inside to feel resentment, but she knew that she should. "I didn't do anything to Tony," she replied coolly. "And the problem is between your brother and me, Michael. Forgive me, but none of this is any of your business."

Michael leaned toward her, his eyes shooting fire. "Do you think I give a damn whether or not you consider this my business? Tony is my brother and I love him!"

Sharon closed her eyes for a moment. She had a headache, probably resulting from the combination of this confrontation and the paint fumes at home. She wanted the whole world to go away and leave her alone—yesterday, if not sooner.

"I salute you, Michael." She sighed, rubbing

her temple with three fingers. "Tony is a hard man to love—I've given up trying."

Michael shoved a strong, sun-browned hand through his curly hair. "Okay," he said in frustration. "I gave it a shot, I blew it. Tony is going to kill me if he ever finds out I came here and told you about last night."

"He won't hear it from me," Sharon assured the young man. "Congratulations on the new contract, by the way. The one for the supermarket."

Michael looked at her curiously for a moment, then got out of his chair. He ran his palms down his thighs in a nervous gesture. "Thanks. Sharon, I just want to say one more thing, and then I'll get out of here. Tony loves you as much as any man has ever loved a woman, and if the two of you don't find a way to reach each other, it's going to be too late."

"It already is," Sharon said with sad conviction. "We shouldn't even have tried."

At that, Michael shook his head and went out. Helen appeared the moment the shop door had closed behind him.

"Are you all right?" she asked.

Sharon shook her head. "No," she answered, "I'm not. Listen, Helen, I have this wretched headache..." *And this broken heart.* "I'd like to leave for the rest of the day. If you don't want to stay, you don't have to—you can just lock up and go home."

Helen was looking at her as though she'd just suggested launching herself from the roof of the mall in a hang glider. "I'll close the shop at the regular time," she said.

Sharon nodded. "Okay, good. Umm—I'll see you tomorrow...."

"Sure," she said with a determined smile. "No hurry, though. I can handle things alone if I have to."

Sharon put on sunglasses, even though it wasn't a particularly bright day, and walked across the parking lot to the roadster. Because she wanted to feel the wind in her face, she put the canvas top down before pulling out of her customary parking space. With no special destination in mind, she drove onto the highway and headed out of town.

She'd been traveling along the freeway for almost an hour before she became aware that she was, after all, definitely going somewhere. She was on her way to Hayesville, the little town on the peninsula where she'd grown up and where her mother still lived.

As huge drops of rain began to fall, Sharon pulled over to the side of the road and, smiling grimly to herself, put the car's top back up. After another hour, she stopped at a restaurant along the roadside to have coffee and call Briana and Matt.

"Where are you, Mom?" Briana wailed. "You're supposed to be with us—it's your turn."

Matt was on one of the other phones. "School starts tomorrow, too," he added.

Sharon closed her eyes for a moment, trying hard to collect herself. It wouldn't do to fall apart in a truck stop and have to be carried back to Port Webster in a basket. "You guys aren't alone, are you? Isn't Mrs. Harry there?"

"No," Bri answered. "Dad is. But he's got a headache, so we're supposed to stay out of the den."

Responsible to the end, Sharon made herself say, "One of you go and tell him to pick up the telephone, please. I have to explain why I can't be there."

While Bri rattled on about her favorite rock group, her prospects of surviving seventh grade and what the orthodontist had said about her friend Mary Kate's broken tooth, Matt went off to the den.

After an eternity of adolescent prattle, Tony came on the line. "Hang up, Briana," he said tersely.

Bri started to protest, then obeyed.

Sharon took the plunge. "Tony, listen to me—"

"No, lady," he broke in brusquely, "you listen to me. I don't know where you are or what you're doing, but it's your turn to hold down the fort, so get your shapely little backside over here and look after these kids!"

Sharon sighed, counted mentally and went on. "I can't. I-I'm out of town."

Tony sounded so cold, like a stranger. "Wonderful. Was your lawyer planning on mentioning that to my lawyer?"

"Don't, Tony," Sharon whispered. "Please, don't be cruel."

"I'm not trying to be. I thought that was the way we were going to be communicating from now on—through our attorneys. God knows, we can't seem to manage a one-to-one conversation."

"That's true, isn't it?" Sharon reflected.

"We're like two incompatible chemicals—we just don't mix."

"Where are you?" Tony asked evenly, after a long and volatile silence.

"I'm going to visit my mother." The words came out sounding stiff, even a little challenging, though Sharon hadn't meant them that way.

"Great," Tony replied. "If you catch her between bingo games, you can pour out your soul."

"That was a rotten thing to say, Tony. Did I make remarks about your mother?"

"Often," he answered.

It was just no damned use. Sharon was glad Tony couldn't see the tears brimming in her eyes. "Give my love to the kids, please, and let them know that I'll be home tomorrow. Tell them we'll have supper out to celebrate their first day of school."

Tony was quiet for so long that Sharon began to think he'd laid the receiver down and walked away. Finally, however, he said, "I'll tell them."

"Thanks," Sharon replied, and then she gently hung up the telephone and went back out to her car.

It was raining hard, and Sharon was glad. The weather was a perfect match for her mood.

7

It was getting dark when Sharon arrived in Hayesville. She turned down Center Street, passing the bank and the feed-and-grain and the filling station, and took a left on Bedford Road.

Her mother lived in a tiny, rented house at the end. The picket fence needed painting, the top of the mailbox was rusted out and the grass was overgrown. Sharon parked in the empty driveway and got out of her car, bringing her purse with her.

She entered through the tattered screen door on the back porch. As always, the key was hanging on its little hook behind the clothes drier; Sharon retrieved it and let herself into her mother's kitchen.

"Bea?" she called once, tentatively, even though she knew she was alone. No doubt, Tony had been right; Bea was playing bingo at the Grange Hall. She only worked part-time as a beautician these days, having acquired some mysterious source of income, which she refused to discuss.

Predictably, there was no answer. Sharon ran a hand through her hair and wondered why she'd driven all this way when she'd known her mother wouldn't be there for her, even if she happened to be physically present.

She looked at the wall phone, wishing that she could call Tony just to hear his voice, and she was startled when it rang. She blinked and then reached out for the receiver. "Hello?"

"Sharon?" Bea's voice sounded cautious, as though she wanted to make sure she was talking to her daughter and not a burglar.

Sharon smiled in spite of everything. "Yes, it's me," she answered quietly. "I just got here."

"Melba Peterson told me she saw you drive by in that fancy yellow car of yours, but I wasn't sure whether to believe her or not. She said they were going to have a thousand-dollar jackpot at bingo tonight, too, and all they've got is a few cases of motor oil and a free lube job at Roy's Texaco."

Sharon twisted one finger in the phone cord. "Does that mean you're coming home?"

Bea was clearly surprised. "Of course I am. Did you think I was just going to let you sit there all by yourself?"

After a moment, Sharon managed to answer, "Yes—I mean, no—"

"I'll be right there, darlin'," Bea announced cheerfully. "Have you had anything to eat?"

"Well—"

"I didn't think so. I'll stop at the burger place on my way home."

Sharon tried again. "I don't really feel—"

"See you in a few minutes," Bea chimed, as though she and her daughter had always been close.

By the time her mother had arrived, roaring up in her exhaust-belching dragon of a car, Sharon had splashed her face with cold water, brushed her hair and mustered a smile.

Bea dashed up the front walk, a grease-dappled white bag in one hand, her purse in the other. "What did he do to you, that big hoodlum?" she demanded, dashing all Sharon's hopes that she'd managed to look normal.

She sighed, holding the screen door open wide as Bea trotted into the living room. "Tony isn't a hoodlum, and he didn't do anything to me—"

"Sure, he didn't. That's why you're up here

in the middle of the week looking like you just lost out on a three-card blackout by one number.'' She gestured with the paper bag, and Sharon followed her into the kitchen.

Bea was a small woman with artfully coiffed hair dyed an improbable shade of champagne blond, and she wore her standard uniform—double-knit slacks, a colorful floral smock and canvas espadrilles. She slapped the burger bag down in the middle of the table and shook one acrylic fingernail under Sharon's nose.

''It's time you let go of that man and found somebody else,'' she lectured.

Sharon was annoyed. ''You never looked for anybody else,'' she pointed out, lingering in the doorway as she'd done so often in her teens, her hands gripping the woodwork.

Bea drew back a chair and sat down, plunging eagerly into the burgers and fries, leaving Sharon the choice between joining her or going hungry. ''What makes you think I needed to look?'' she asked after a few moments.

Sharon sat and reached for a cheeseburger. ''You mean you had a romance in your life and I didn't even know it?''

Bea smiled and tapped the tabletop with one of her formidable pink nails. ''There was a lot you didn't know, sweetheart," she said smugly. Then she laughed at her daughter's wide-eyed expression.

The two of them sat in companionable silence for several minutes, consuming their suppers. Finally, Sharon blurted out, "I'm still in love with Tony."

"Tell me something I didn't already know," Bea answered with a sigh.

Sharon's throat had closed; she laid down what remained of her cheeseburger and sat staring at it. "I guess you were right when you said it would never work," she said, when she could get the words out.

Bea's hand, glittering with cheap rings, rose hesitantly to cover hers. "I didn't want you to be hurt," she answered gently. "Tony was young, he'd just lost his wife, he had a little baby to raise. I was afraid he was going to use you."

"But you said—"

"I know what I said. I told you that he was out of your league. That he'd get tired of you."

Sharon was watching her mother, unable to speak. This understanding, sympathetic Bea wasn't the woman she remembered; she didn't know how to respond.

"I was hoping to discourage you," Bea confessed, a faraway expression in her eyes. "It was never easy for you and me to talk, was it?"

"No," Sharon said with a shake of her head. "It wasn't."

Bea smiled sadly. "I didn't know how," she said. "We didn't have Phil Donahue and Oprah Winfrey to tell us things like that when you were a girl."

Sharon turned her hand so that she could grip her mother's. "How's this for talking?" she asked hoarsely. "I can't think anymore, Bea— all I seem to be able to do is feel. And everything hurts."

"That's love, all right," Bea remarked. "Do you have any idea how Tony feels?"

Sharon shook her head. "No. Sometimes I think he loves me, but then something happens and everything goes to hell in the proverbial hand basket."

"What do you mean, 'something happens'?"

Dropping her eyes, Sharon said, "Yesterday I got this bright idea that I was going to surprise Tony with a real Italian dinner. Only I was the one who got the surprise."

Bea squeezed her hand. "Go on."

She related how she'd stumbled upon the pictures of Carmen with the votive candle burning reverently in front of them.

"There was probably an explanation for that," Bea observed. "It doesn't sound like the kind of thing Tony would do, especially after all this time."

Sharon bit into her lower lip for a moment. "I know that now," she whispered miserably.

"You couldn't just go back and apologize? Or call him?"

"Tony has a way of distancing himself from me," Sharon mused with a distracted shake of her head. "It hurts too much."

"It would probably be safe to assume that you've hurt him a time or two," Bea reasoned. "Didn't you tell me once that Tony went into a rage when you divorced him?"

Sharon closed her eyes at the memory, nodding. She'd never once been afraid of Tony, not until that day when he'd come into Teddy Bares with the divorce papers in his hand, looking as though he could kill without hesitation. She'd stood proudly behind the counter, trembling inside, afraid to tell him why she couldn't remain married to him—and not sure she knew the answer herself.

Bea spoke softly. "You say you love Tony,

but it would be my guess that you still don't understand what's going on between the two of you. Well, you were right before, Sharon—you don't dare go back to him until you know what went wrong in the first place.''

''What can I do?'' Sharon whispered, feeling broken inside. She ached to be held in Tony's arms again, to lie beside him in bed at night, to laugh with him and fight with him.

''Wait,'' Bea counseled. ''Try to give yourself some space so that you'll be able to think a little more clearly. If you love a man, it's next to impossible to be objective when you're too close.''

''How did you get so smart?'' Sharon asked with a tearful smile.

Bea shrugged, but she looked pleased at the compliment. ''By making mistakes, I suppose.'' She got up to start brewing coffee in her shiny electric percolator.

Sharon gathered up the debris from their casual dinner and tossed it into the trash, then wiped the tabletop clean with a damp sponge.

''Tony's not such a bad man,'' Bea said in a quiet voice. ''I guess I just have a tendency to dislike him because he has so much power to hurt you.''

Sharon looked at her mother in silence. Their relationship was a long way from normal, but at least they were both making an effort to open up and be honest about what they thought and felt.

That night she slept in her own familiar room. When she awakened the next morning, she felt a little better, a little stronger.

Sharon found Bea in the kitchen, making breakfast. As Bea fried bacon, she told her daughter all about the new car she intended to win at that day's bingo session. And then the telephone rang.

Pouring two cups of fresh coffee, as well as keeping an eye on the bacon, Sharon listened while her mother answered with a bright hello. "Yes, she's here," she said after a moment of silence. "Just a moment."

Sharon turned, smoothing her skirt with nervous hands, and gave her mother a questioning look.

"It's Mr. Morelli—Vincent," Bea whispered, holding the receiver against her bosom.

Some premonition made Sharon pull back a chair and sit down before speaking to her former father-in-law. "Vincent?" she asked, and her voice shook.

The gentle voice thrummed with sadness and fear. "I have bad news for you, sweetheart," Vincent began, and Sharon groped for Bea's hand. It was there for her to grip, strong and certain. "There was an accident early this morning, and Tony's been hurt. The doctors still don't know how bad it is."

The familiar kitchen seemed to sway and shift. Sharon squeezed her eyes shut for a second in an effort to ground herself. "What happened?" she managed to get out.

Vincent sighed, and the sound conveyed grief, frustration, anger. "Tonio was climbing the framework on one of the sites, and he fell. He wasn't wearing a safety belt."

Sharon swallowed, envisioning the accident all too clearly in her mind. "Are Briana and Matt all right?"

"They're at school," Vincent answered. "They haven't been told. The rest of the family is here at City Hospital."

"I'll be there as soon as I possibly can," Sharon said. "And Vincent? Thank you for calling me."

"Thank heaven the housekeeper knew where you were. Drive carefully, little one—we don't need another accident."

Sharon promised to be cautious, but even as she hung up she was looking around wildly for her purse. She was confused and frantic, and tears were slipping down her cheeks.

Bea forced her to stand still by gripping both of Sharon's hands in her own. "Tell me. One of the children has been hurt?"

Sharon shook her head. "No—it's Tony. He fell—the doctors don't know…" She pulled one hand free of her mother's and raised it to her forehead. "Oh, God, it will take me hours to get there—my purse! Where is my purse?"

Bea took the purse from the top of the dishwasher and opened it without hesitation, taking out Sharon's car keys. "I'm driving—you're too upset," she announced.

Minutes later Bea was at the wheel of the expensive yellow roadster, speeding out of town, her daughter sitting numbly in the passenger seat.

Sharon nearly collided with Michael when she came through the entrance of the hospital; in fact, she would have if her brother-in-law hadn't reached out with both hands to prevent it.

"Tony…?" she choked out, because that was all she could manage. She knew that her eyes were taking up her whole face and that she was pale.

Michael's expression was tender. "He's going to be all right," he said quickly, eager to reassure her, still supporting her with his hands.

Relief swept over Sharon in a wave that weakened her knees and brought a strangled little cry to her throat. "Thank God," she whispered. And then, in a fever of joy, she threw her arms around Michael's neck.

He held her until she stepped back, sniffling, to ask, "Where is he? I want to see him."

Michael's dark eyes were full of pain. "I don't think that would be a good idea, princess," he said, his voice sounding husky. "Not right now."

"Where is he?" Sharon repeated, this time in a fierce whisper. Her entire body was stiff with determination.

Michael sighed. "Room 229. But, Sharon—"

Sharon was already moving toward the elevator. Bea, still parking the car, would have to find her own way through the maze that was City Hospital.

Room 229 was in a corner, and members of the Morelli family were overflowing into the hallway. Sharon was glad she'd encountered Michael before coming upstairs, or she might have thought that the worst had happened.

News of her arrival buzzed through the group of well-wishers, and they stepped aside to admit her.

Tony was sitting up in bed with a bandage wrapped around his head. His face was bruised and scraped, and his left arm was in a cast. But it was the look in his eyes that stopped Sharon in the middle of the room.

His expression was cold, as though he hated her.

Vincent and Maria, who had been standing on the other side of the room, silently withdrew. Sharon knew without looking around that the other visitors had left, also.

And she was still stuck in the middle of the floor with her heart jammed in her throat. She had to swallow twice before she could speak. ''I got here as quickly as I could,'' she said huskily. ''Are—are you all right?''

Tony only nodded, the intensity of his anger plainly visible in his eyes.

A cold wind blew over Sharon's soul. ''Tony—''

''Stay away,'' he said, shifting his gaze, at last, to the window. In the distance the waters of the sound shimmered and sparkled in the afternoon sun. "Please—just stay away."

Sharon couldn't move. She wanted to run to him; at the same time, she needed to escape. "I'm not going anywhere until you tell me what's the matter," she told him. The moment the words were out of her mouth, she wondered if she'd really said them herself, since they sounded so reasonable and poised.

Tony was still looking out the window. "We cause each other too much pain," he said after a long time.

She dared to take a step closer to the bed. Her hands ached to touch Tony, to soothe and lend comfort, but she kept them stiffly at her sides. His words, true though they were, struck her with the aching sting of small pelted stones.

Sharon waited in silence, knowing there was nothing to do but wait and endure until he'd said everything.

"We have to stop living in the past and go on with our lives. Today taught me that, if nothing else."

There were tears burning in Sharon's eyes; she lowered her head to hide them and bit into her lower lip.

"You can have the house," he went on mer-

cilessly. At last Tony looked at Sharon; she
could feel his gaze touching her. His voice was
a harsh, grinding rasp. "I've never been able to
sleep in our room. Did you know that?"

Sharon shook her head; pride forced her to lift
it. "I've slept in the den a lot of times myself,"
she confessed.

The ensuing silence was awful. Unable to bear
it, Sharon went boldly to the side of the bed even
though she knew she wouldn't be welcome.

"I was so scared," she whispered. Her hand
trembled as she reached out to touch the bandage
encircling his head. It hid most of his hair and
dipped down on one side over his eye, giving
him a rakish look.

"No doubt," Tony said with cruel dryness,
"you were afraid that Carmen and I had found
a way to be together at last."

The gibe was a direct hit. Sharon allowed the
pain to rock her, her eyes never shifting from
Tony's. Speech, for the moment, was more than
she could manage.

"The 'shrine,' as you called it, was my grandmother's doing," Tony went on, with a terrible
humor twisting one side of his mouth and flickering in his eyes. "I'd talked Mama into giving
up the pictures, since they bothered you so

much. I planned on turning them over to Bri later on, when she and I were getting along a little better. In the meantime, Grandmama found them. Evidently, she decided to while away the time by honoring the dead.''

Sharon lifted her index finger to his lips in a plea for silence, because she could bear no more. He was right—so right. They were causing each other too much pain.

She grasped at a slightly less volatile subject with the desperation of a drowning woman. ''What about Bri? Will I still be able to see her?''

Tony looked at her as though she'd struck him. ''You're the only mother she's ever known. I wouldn't hurt her—or you—by keeping the two of you apart.''

''Thank you,'' Sharon said in a shattered whisper. She touched his lips very gently with her own. ''Rest now,'' she told him, just before she turned to walk away.

He grasped her arm to stop her, and when she looked back over one shoulder, she saw that his eyes were bright with tears. ''Goodbye,'' he said.

Sharon put a hand to her mouth in an effort to control her own emotions and ran out of the room. The hallway was empty except for her father-in-law.

Vincent took one look at Sharon and drew her into his arms. "There, there," he said softly. "Everything will be all right now. Tonio will be well and strong."

The sobs Sharon had been holding back came pouring out. She let her forehead rest against Vincent's shoulder and gave way to all her grief and confusion and pain.

"Tell me, little one," he urged gently when the worst was over. "Tell me what hurts you so much."

Sharon looked up at him and tried to smile. Ignoring his request, she said instead, "Tony is so lucky to have a father like you." She stood on tiptoe and kissed Vincent's weathered, sun-browned cheek, and that was her farewell.

Bea, who had been in the waiting room with Maria, came toward Sharon as she pushed the button to summon the elevator. Neither woman spoke until they'd found the roadster in the parking lot and Sharon had slid behind the wheel, holding out her hand to Bea for the keys.

With a shake of her head, Bea got into the car on the passenger side and surrendered them. "Where are we going now?"

Sharon started the car and then dried her cheeks with the heels of her palms. Before backing out of the parking space, she snapped her seat belt in place. "Home," she replied. "We're going home. Tony just gave me the house."

"He just what?" Bea demanded. "The man is giving away his possessions? Tony's own mother told me, not fifteen minutes ago, that he's going to be fine. They're letting him leave the hospital tomorrow."

Sharon was concentrating on the traffic flow moving past the hospital. If she didn't, she was sure she would fall apart. "The house isn't his 'possession,' Mother. It belonged to both of us."

Sharon had addressed Bea by a term other than her given name for the first time in fifteen years; she knew that had to have some significance, but she was too overwrought to figure out what it was.

"If it's all the same to you," Bea said, when they were moving toward Tamarack Drive, "I'd like to go home tomorrow. I could take the bus."

Sharon only nodded; she would have agreed to almost anything at that point.

The moment the car pulled into the driveway, Bri and Matt came bursting out the front door, still wearing their first-day-of-school clothes. They were closely followed by Rose, who was resting both hands on her protruding stomach.

Sharon addressed her former sister-in-law first. "He's all right—you knew that, didn't you?"

Rose nodded. "Papa called. It's you we're worried about."

Bri and Matt were both hugging Sharon, and she laughed hoarsely as she tried to hold each one at the same time.

"Mom, is Daddy really okay?" Briana demanded, when they were all in the kitchen moments later.

Sharon was careful not to meet the child's eyes. "Yes, babe. He's fine."

"Then why isn't he here?" Matt wanted to know. He was staying closer to her than usual; Sharon understood his need for reassurance because she felt it, too.

"They want to keep him in the hospital overnight, probably just to be on the safe side," Sharon told her son. "He's got a broken arm, a few cuts and scrapes and a bandage on his head. Other than that, he seems to be fine."

"Honest?" Bri pressed.

"Honest," Sharon confirmed. "Now, I want to hear all about your first day of school."

Both children began to talk at once, and Sharon had to intercede with a patient, "One at a time. Who wants to be first?"

Bri generously allowed her brother that consideration, and Matt launched into a moment-by-moment account of his day.

Much later, when dinner was over and both Bri and Matt had gone upstairs to their rooms, Sharon made out the sofa bed in the den for her mother. She was like an automaton, doing everything by rote.

Bea retired immediately.

Wanting a cup of herbal tea before bed, Sharon returned to the kitchen and was surprised to find that Michael had let himself in. He was leaning against a counter, his arms folded, just as Sharon had seen Tony do so many times. As a matter of fact, the resemblance was startling.

"I tried to warn you that Tony was in that kind of mood," Michael said kindly, his eyes full of sympathy and caring. Sharon reflected again that Tony was fortunate—not only did he have Vincent for a father, he had a whole network of people who truly loved him.

"Yes," Sharon replied in a small voice. "You did."

"Whatever he said," Michael persisted, "he didn't mean it."

Sharon longed to be alone. "You weren't there to hear," she answered. And then she turned and went upstairs, hoping that Michael would understand.

She had no more strength left.

8

Sharon found her passport in the bottom of a drawer of her desk at home, jammed behind some of Tony's old tax records and canceled checks, which she promptly dropped. Kneeling on the floor and muttering, she began gathering up the scattered papers.

That was when she saw the check made out to her mother. Tony had signed it with a flourish, and the date was only a few weeks in the past.

Frowning, Sharon began to sort through the other checks. She soon deduced that Tony had virtually been supporting Bea for years.

Having forgotten her passport completely by this time, Sharon got to her feet and reached for the telephone. It was early on a Saturday morning and, unless Tony had changed considerably since their divorce, he would be sleeping in.

Sharon had no compunction at all about waking him. She hadn't seen Tony, except from an upstairs window when he picked up the kids, in nearly two months. She also avoided talking to him on the telephone, although that was harder.

She supposed this was some kind of turning point.

A woman answered the phone, and Sharon closed her eyes for a moment. She hadn't expected to feel that achy hurt deep down inside herself, not after all this time. "Is Tony there, please?"

"Who's calling?" retorted the voice. Sharon wondered if she was speaking to the infamous blonde of Michael's mentioning. She also wondered if the woman had spent the night with Tony.

"I'm Sharon Morelli," she said warmly. "Who are you?"

"My name is Ingrid," came the matter-of-fact response.

Yep, Sharon thought miserably. *It's the blonde. People named Ingrid are always blond.* "I'd like to speak to Tony," she reminded his friend with consummate dignity.

"Right," Ingrid answered. "Hey, Tony—it's your ex-wife."

"Bimbo," Sharon muttered.

"I beg your pardon?" Ingrid responded politely.

Tony came on the line before Sharon had to reply, and he sounded worried. In fact, he didn't even bother to say hello. "Is everything all right?" he wanted to know.

Sharon looked down at the assortment of checks in her hand. "Since when do you support my mother?" she countered.

He sighed. "She told you," he said, sounding resigned.

"Hell no," Sharon swore, her temper flaring. And it wasn't just the checks; it was Ingrid, and a lot of other problems. "Nobody around here tells me anything!"

"Calm down," Tony told her in reasonable tones. "You don't begrudge Bea the money, do you?"

"Of course not," Sharon said crisply.

"Then what's the problem?"

"You didn't mention it, that's what. I mean a little thing like supporting someone usually comes up in day-to-day husband-and-wife conversation, doesn't it?"

"We aren't husband and wife," Tony pointed out.

"Damn it, we were when you started writing

these checks every month. And neither you nor Bea said a word!''

''Sorry. Guess we were just trying to maintain our images, having convinced everybody that we didn't like each other.''

Sharon sighed and sagged into a chair. Sometimes it was so frustrating to talk to this man, but in a way it felt good, too. ''Are you still sending my mother money every month?'' she asked straight-out.

''Yes,'' Tony answered just as succinctly.

''I want you to stop. If Bea needs financial help, I'll take care of it.''

''That's very independent and liberated of you, but the thing is out of your hands. My accountants see to it every month—like the child support.''

Sharon drew in a deep breath and let it out again. Then she repeated the exercise. In, out, in, out. She would not let Tony short-circuit her composure; she'd grown beyond that in the past two months. ''Bea is not a child,'' she said.

''That,'' Tony immediately retorted, ''is a matter of opinion. I think we need to talk about this in person.''

Sharon was filled with sweet alarm. She'd stayed out of Tony's range since that day in the hospital, and she wasn't sure she was ready to be in the same room with him. On the other hand, the idea had a certain appeal. "I'm busy," she hedged.

Too late Sharon realized how thin that argument was. In truth, with all the help she'd hired at Teddy Bares, she had more time on her hands than she was used to.

"Doing what?" The question, of course, was inevitable. It was also a measure of Tony Morelli's innate gall.

Sharon's eyes fell on the blue cover of her passport. She smiled as she spoke. "I'm getting ready to go to Paris on a buying trip, actually."

"The kids didn't mention that," Tony said, and the statement had a faint air of complaint to it.

So Bri and Matt were making reports when they visited their dad, just as they did when they came home to Sharon. Well, it figured.

She smiled harder. "They don't tell you everything, I'm sure."

Tony was quiet for a few moments, absorbing that. "What should they be telling me that they aren't?" he finally asked.

Sharon wound her finger in the phone cord, hoping to sound distracted, disinterested. "Oh, this and that," she said. "Nothing important. I know you're busy, so I won't keep you." With that, she summarily hung up.

Twenty-two minutes later, Tony entered the den. Sharon noted, out of the corner of her eye, that he was wearing jeans, a T-shirt and a running jacket. Tony was especially attractive when he was about to work out.

"Hi," he said somewhat sheepishly.

Sharon smiled. She knew he'd just realized that he'd forgotten to come up with an excuse for dropping by. She looked up from the ledgers for Teddy Bares, which she always liked to check before they went to the accountant. "Hi, Tony." There was a cheerful fire crackling in the den's large brick fireplace, and the radio was tuned to an easy-listening station. "I see they took off your cast."

Tony sighed and then nodded, jamming his hands into the pockets of his navy-blue jacket. "Are the kids around?"

Briana and Matt were on the island staying in the A-frame with Tony's sister Gina and her husband. And Tony knew that.

"No," Sharon answered, refraining from pointing up the fact.

Still, he lingered. "Isn't November kind of a rotten time to go to Paris?" he finally asked.

Sharon looked down at her ledgers to hide a grin. "There is no such thing as a 'rotten time to go to Paris,'" she commented.

Tony went into the kitchen and came back with two mugs of coffee—one of which he somewhat grudgingly set down on the surface of Sharon's desk. "We went there on our honeymoon," he said, as if that had some bearing on Sharon's plans.

"I know," she replied dryly.

"The Bahamas would be warmer."

"They're not showing the spring lingerie lines in the Bahamas," was the reasonable reply. Sharon still hadn't looked up into those brown eyes; if she did that, she'd be lost.

Tony went to stand in front of the fire, his broad, powerful back turned to Sharon. "I guess we still haven't learned to talk to each other," he observed.

Sharon hadn't even realized that she'd been playing a game until he spoke. "I thought we'd given up on that," she said, in a soft voice that betrayed some of the sadness she felt.

"I've always found it difficult to do that,"

Tony remarked somewhat distantly. "Give up, I mean. Are you going to the company party?"

The mention of the celebration Vincent and Maria held every year just before Thanksgiving brought Ingrid to Sharon's mind. "I was invited," she said, avoiding his eyes. With the speed of Matt's hamsters fleeing their cage, her next words got out before she could stop them. "Are you taking Ingrid?"

There was an element of thunder in Tony's silence. "Yes," he answered after a very long time.

I've done it again, Sharon thought to herself. *I've asked a question I didn't want to have answered.* "If I have time, what with my trip to Paris," she told him, putting on a front, "I'll probably drop by."

"Good," Tony answered. His coffee mug made a solid thump sound as he set it down. "I'd better get to the gym, I guess," he added as a taut afterthought.

Sharon pretended a devout interest in the figures in her ledgers, although in reality they had about as much meaning for her as Chinese characters. "Aren't you forgetting something?"

"What?" he challenged in a vaguely belligerent tone. Sharon knew without looking that he'd thrust his hands into his jacket pockets again.

"We didn't discuss your sending money to Bea. I don't like it—it makes me feel obligated." At last she trusted herself to meet his eyes.

Quiet fury altered Tony's expression. "Why the hell should it do that? Have I asked you for anything?"

Sharon shook her head, stunned by the sheer force of his annoyance. "No, but—"

He folded his arms, and his dark eyes were still snapping. "I can afford to help Bea and I want to. That's the end of it," he said flatly.

Sharon sighed. "It isn't your responsibility to look after my mother," she told him gently. "I don't even understand why you feel it's necessary."

"You wouldn't," Tony retorted, his tone clipped, and then he walked out.

The festive feeling that autumn days often fostered in Sharon was gone. She propped both elbows on the surface of her desk and rested her forehead in her palms.

At least he hadn't made her cry this time. She figured that was some sort of progress.

* * *

"You've got to go to that party!" Helen said sternly, resting her arms on the counter and leaning toward Sharon with an earnest expression in her eyes. It had been a busy day, and they were getting ready to turn Teddy Bares over to Louise, the middle-aged saleswoman Sharon had hired to work from five-thirty until nine o'clock when the mall closed. "Furthermore, you have to take a date that will set Tony Morelli back on his heels!"

"Where am I going to get someone like that?" Sharon asked, a little annoyed that the dating game was so easy for Tony to play and so difficult for her. She'd been out with exactly four men since the divorce, and all of them were duds.

Helen was thoughtfully tapping her chin as she thought. A moment later her face was shining with revelation. "You could ask Michael to help you."

Sharon frowned, nonplussed. "Tony's brother?"

"He must know a lot of terrific guys, being pretty spectacular himself."

"Yeah," Sharon said wryly. "For instance, he knows Tony. He'd go straight to big brother and spill his guts. I can hear it now. 'Tonio,

Sharon is so desperate that she's after me to fix her up with blind dates.' No way, Helen!''

Helen shrugged. ''I'm only trying to help. It's too bad you don't have the kind of business where you might meet more men.''

''I wouldn't want one who shopped at Teddy Bares,'' Sharon remarked with a grin. ''He'd either be married or very weird.''

Helen made a face. ''You are no help at all. I'm going to ask Allen what he can dig up at the gym.''

Sharon winced at the thought of Helen's husband approaching strange men and asking them what they were doing on the night of the twenty-second. It could get him punched out, for one thing. ''Thanks, but no thanks. I don't like jocks.''

''Tony's a jock,'' Helen pointed out. ''Or are those washboard stomach muscles of his an illusion?''

''When,'' Sharon demanded loftily, holding back a smile, ''did you happen to get a look at my ex-husband's stomach, pray tell?''

Helen batted her lashes and tried to look wicked. ''Fourth of July picnic, two years ago, on Vashon. Remember the volleyball game?''

Sharon remembered, all right. Tony had been

wearing cutoffs and a half shirt, and every time he'd jumped for the ball...

She began to feel too warm.

Helen gave her an impish look and went to the back room for their coats and purses. When she came out again, Louise had arrived to take over.

"I'm going to ask Allen to check out the jocks," Helen insisted, as she and Sharon walked out of the mall together.

Sharon lifted her chin a degree. "I might not be back from Paris in time for the party anyway, so don't bother."

"Maybe you'll meet somebody on the plane," Helen speculated.

Sharon rolled her eyes and strode off toward her car. When she got home, a surprise awaited her.

Maria was sitting at the kitchen table, chatting with Bri and Matt. Mrs. Harry had evidently been so charmed that she'd not only stayed late, she was serving tea.

She said a pleasant good-night and left when Sharon came in, and the kids, after collecting their hugs, ran off to watch TV in the den.

Sharon had a suspicion that their disappearance had been prearranged. "Hello, Maria. It's good to see you." She realized with a start that she'd meant those words.

Maria returned Sharon's smile. "I hope I haven't come at a bad time."

"You're always welcome, of course," Sharon replied with quiet sincerity. Mrs. Harry had started dinner—there was a casserole in the oven—so she had nothing to do but take off her coat, hang it up and pour herself a cup of tea.

She sat down at the table with Maria, who looked uncomfortable now, and even a little shy.

"I've come to ask if you were planning to attend our party," the older woman said softly. "Vincent and I are so hoping that you will. We don't see enough of you, Sharon."

Sharon was taken aback. "I'm not sure if I can come or not," she answered. "You see, I'm traveling to Paris that week."

Maria seemed genuinely disappointed. "That's exciting," she said, and she sounded so utterly insincere that Sharon had to smile. Her former mother-in-law smiled, too. Sharon had never noticed before now how sweet it made her look.

Sharon knew her eyes were dancing as she took a sip of her tea. "It's important to you that I come to the party, but I'm not sure why."

Maria looked down at her lap. "I guess I'm trying to make amends—however belatedly. I realize now that I didn't treat you as well as I could have, and I regret it."

Sharon reached out to touch Maria's hand. "I have regrets, too," she said. "I didn't try very hard to understand how you must have loved Carmen."

Maria swallowed and nodded. "She was like my own child, but I should have made you feel more like a part of our family. Forgive me, please, for letting an old grief stand in the way of the friendship we could have had."

Sharon felt tears sting her eyes. "There's nothing to forgive," she replied. After a short interval had passed, she added, "You know, Maria, if I could be the kind of mother to Matt and Briana that you were to your children, I'd count myself a resounding success."

The compliment brought a flush of pleasure to Maria's porcelain-smooth cheeks and a gentle brightness to her eyes. She was of another generation; her life revolved around her husband, children and grandchildren. "What a wonderful thing to say," she whispered. "Thank you."

Sharon leaned forward, her hand still resting on Maria's. "They're all so self-assured and strong, from Tony right down to Michael and Rose. What's your secret?''

Maria looked surprised. ''Why, I simply loved them,'' she answered. ''The way you love Briana and Matthew.'' She paused and smiled mischievously. ''And, of course, I had the good sense to marry Vincent Morelli in the first place. The self-assurance—as you call it—comes from him, I'm sure. And there have been times when I would have used another word for what my children have—brass. They can be obnoxious.''

Before Sharon could agree that Tony, at least, had been known to suffer from that condition, there was a brief rap at the back door and he came strolling into the kitchen. He spared his ex-wife a glance, crossed the room and bent to give his mother a kiss on the cheek.

Bri and Matt, having heard his car, came racing into the room, full of joy. Tony was always greeted like a conquering hero, there to save the two of them from a death too horrible to contemplate, and that was a sore spot with Sharon.

''Hi,'' she said to him, when the hubbub had died down a little.

''Hello,'' he responded quietly.

Guilt struck Sharon full force. It was getting late, and Mrs. Harry's casserole was probably shriveling in the oven. She left her chair and hurried over to pull it out.

"Won't you stay to dinner, Maria?" she asked. Then, hesitantly, she added, "Tony?"

Both potential guests shook their heads. "Vincent and I are meeting downtown at our favorite restaurant," Maria said. "In fact, if I don't hurry, I'll be late."

With that, she went through a round of farewells including Tony, Briana, Matt, and finally, Sharon. "Don't let him push you around," she whispered to her former daughter-in-law, squeezing her hand.

Sharon grinned and, when Maria was gone, turned her attention to Tony. "Okay, what's your excuse, Morelli? Why can't you stay for dinner?"

"Because I hate Scary Harry's tuna-bean surprise, that's why," he answered. "Last time I had it, it was worse than a surprise—it was a shock."

Naturally, the kids took up the chorus.

"Tuna-bean surprise?" wailed Bri, with all the pathos of a person asked to eat kitty litter. "Yech!"

"Can't we go out?" Matt added.

"See what you started?" Sharon said, frowning at Tony. "Thanks a lot."

Tony slid his hands into the pockets of his jeans and rocked back on the heels of his boots, looking pleased with himself. "I could always take the three of you out for dinner," he suggested innocently.

Bri and Matt were beside themselves at the prospect. "Please, Mom?" they begged in pitiful unison. "Please?"

Sharon was glaring now. "That was a dirty trick," she said to Tony. "It would serve all of you right if I said no." She paused, glancing down at the concoction Mrs. Harry had left in the oven. It did have a surprising aspect about it.

"She's weakening," Tony told the kids.

Sharon tried for a stern look. "Did you two finish your homework?"

Both Briana and Matt nodded, their eyes bright with eagerness.

She shrugged. "Then what can I possibly say," she began, spreading her hands, "except yes?"

Two minutes later they were all in Tony's car. "Put on your seat belts," he said over one shoulder, and Bri and Matt immediately obeyed.

Sharon wondered how he managed to elicit such ready cooperation. She always had to plead, reason, quote statistics and, finally, threaten in order to achieve what Tony had with a mere five words.

When they'd reached the restaurant and the kids were occupied with their all-time favorite food, spaghetti, he turned to Sharon and asked, "Are you really going to Paris?"

She looked down at the swirl of pasta on the end of her fork. Maybe it was wrong of her, given the fact that their marriage was over, but she was glad that he cared what she did. "Yes," she answered. Only superhuman effort—and the presence of her children—kept her from countering, *Are you sleeping with Ingrid?*

An awkward silence fell, and Tony was the one who finally broke it.

"Remember when we were there?" he asked quietly.

There was a lump in Sharon's throat. Vincent and Maria had given them the trip as a wedding present, and it had been like something out of a fairy tale. "How could I forget?" she asked in a voice that was barely audible. She hadn't thought, until now, how many bittersweet memories would be there to meet her once she arrived in France.

"Sharon?"

She lifted her eyes and met his gaze questioningly.

"If I said the wrong thing again," he told her, "I'm sorry."

She swallowed and worked up a smile. "You didn't," she answered, marveling at herself because if he'd asked to go along on the trip to Paris, she would have agreed with delight.

Only Tony wasn't going to ask because he had Ingrid now and he'd only been trying to make conversation in the first place. He probably wasn't even interested in Sharon's plans.

She thought of how Tony would react if she told him that she was considering opening a second shop in nearby Tacoma and winced at the memories that came to mind. A fairly modern man in most respects, he'd reverted to the Neanderthal mind-set when Sharon had opened Teddy Bares, and things had gotten progressively worse....

Tony started to reach for her hand, then hesitated. Although he said nothing, his eyes asked her a thousand questions.

She looked at him sadly. If only he'd been proud of her, she reflected, things might have turned out so differently.

9

The red-sequined dress was long and slinky with a plunging neckline and a sexy slit up one side, and it looked spectacular on Sharon.

"I can't afford it," she whispered to Helen, who was shopping with her while Louise looked after Teddy Bares. The two women were standing in the special occasions section of the best department store in the mall, gazing at Sharon's reflection in a mirror.

"Tony's going to fall into the punch bowl when he sees you," Helen responded, as though Sharon hadn't said anything.

Sharon squinted and threw her shoulders back. "Do you think it makes me look taller?"

Helen nodded solemnly. "Oh, yes," she answered.

With a sigh, Sharon calculated the purchasing power remaining on her credit card—the margin had narrowed considerably after the divorce, and if she bought this dress, it would take her to her limit. "I haven't even got a date," she reflected aloud, speaking as much to herself as to Helen.

"Have a little faith, will you? Allen's checking out the hunks up at the gym—it's a matter of time, that's all."

"A matter of time until he gets his teeth rearranged, you mean."

Helen shook her head, a half smile on her face. "Stop worrying and buy the dress. If our plans don't work out, you can always return it."

The logic of that was irrefutable. Sharon returned to the dressing room to change back into her slacks and blouse and when that was done, she bought the dress. She and Helen parted company then, and Sharon hurried home.

The kids were in the kitchen obediently doing their homework, and something good was baking in the oven. "I've got it," Sharon said, bending to kiss Briana's cheek and then Matt's. "I've been caught in a time warp or something and flung into a rerun of *The Donna Reed Show*, right?"

Bri gave her a look of affectionate disdain. "Mrs. Harry had to leave early—she lost a filling and needed to go to the dentist. She tried to call you at the shop, but you were gone, so—"

"So your dad came over to pinch-hit," Sharon guessed. The prospect of encountering Tony now made her feel a festive sort of despondency. "Where is he?"

As if in answer to that, Tony came out of the den. He was wearing jeans and a dark blue velour pullover, and his eyes slid over Sharon at their leisure, causing her a delightful discomfort. He strolled casually over to the wall oven and checked on whatever it was that smelled so marvelous. "Been shopping for your trip?" he asked.

Sharon realized that she was still holding the dress box from her favorite department store and self-consciously set it aside. "Not exactly," she said, with an exuberance that rang false even in her own ears. "How have you been, Tony?"

"Just terrific," he answered, with an ironic note in his voice as he closed the oven door. "Somebody named Sven called. He said Bea gave him your number."

Sven? Sharon searched her memory, but the only Sven she could come up with was a Swedish exchange student who had spent a year in Hayesville long ago when she'd still been in high school. "Did he leave a message?" she asked airily, wanting to let Tony wonder a little.

"He said he'd call back," Tony answered off-handedly. Sharon knew that he was watching her out of the corner of his eye as he took plates from a cupboard. "Your accountant wants a word with you, too."

Sharon was careful not to show the concern that fact caused her. Her accountant never called unless the news was bad.

At some unseen signal from her father, Matt and Bri had put aside their homework, and they were now setting the table. "You're supposed to call her at home," Tony added. He washed his hands at the sink, took some plastic bags of produce from the refrigerator and began tearing lettuce leaves for a salad.

Sharon was really fretting now, though she smiled brightly. She took off her coat and hung it up, then went upstairs with the box under her arm. The moment she reached the sanctity of the bedroom, she lunged for the telephone and took the directory from the nightstand drawer.

Moments later she was on the line with Susan Fenwick, her accountant. "What do you mean I can't afford to go to Paris?" she whispered in horror. "This is a business trip—"

"I don't care," Susan interrupted firmly. "You've got quarterly taxes coming up, Sharon, and even though you've been gaining some ground financially, you're going to put yourself in serious jeopardy if you make any major expenditures now.''

Sharon sighed. She'd told everyone that she was going to Paris—Tony, the kids, Helen and Louise...just everyone. She was going to look like a real fool, backing out now.

''Okay,'' she said, forcing herself to smile. She'd heard once in a seminar that a businessperson should keep a pleasant expression on her face while talking on the telephone. ''Thank you, Susan.''

''No problem. I'm sorry about the trip. Maybe in the spring—''

''Right,'' Sharon said. ''Goodbye.''

Susan returned the sentiment and then the line was dead.

Sharon hung up and went downstairs, the smile firmly affixed to her face. The kids were already eating and Tony was in the den, gathering up the ever-present blueprints.

''Are those the plans for the new supermarket?'' Sharon asked, wanting that most elusive of things—a nonvolatile conversation with Tony.

He nodded, and it seemed to Sharon that he

was avoiding her eyes. "The kids are having supper," he said. "Don't you want to join them?"

"I'm not hungry," Sharon answered with a slight shake of her head. In truth she was ravenous, but that fabulous, slinky dress didn't leave room for indulgences in Tony's cooking. Once he was gone, she'd have a salad.

Tony's gaze swung toward her, assessing her. "Trying to slim down to Parisian standards?" he asked dryly.

Sharon longed to tell him that the trip was off, that she couldn't afford to go, but her pride wouldn't allow her to make the admission. Her need to make a mark on the world had been a pivotal factor in their divorce, and Sharon didn't want to call attention to the fact that her standard of living had gone down since they'd parted ways. She let Tony's question pass. "Thank you for coming over and taking care of the kids," she said.

"Anytime," he responded quietly. There was a forlorn expression in Tony's eyes even as he smiled that made Sharon want to cross the room and put her arms around that lean, fit waist of his. The desire to close the space between them, both physically and emotionally, was powerful indeed.

Sharon resisted it. "Did Sven leave a number?" she asked in a soft voice, to deflect the sweet, impossible charge she felt coursing back and forth between herself and this man she loved but could not get along with.

Tony looked tired, and his sigh was on the ragged side. His grin, however, was crooked and made of mischief with a pinch of acid thrown in for spice. "It isn't tattooed on your body somewhere?" he countered.

Color throbbing in her face, Sharon ran a hand through her hair and did her best to ignore Tony as she went past him to the desk. A number was scrawled on a pad beside the telephone, along with a notation about Susan's call. Conflicting needs tore at her; she wanted to pound on Tony with her fists, and at the same time she longed to make love to him.

She was startled when he turned her into his embrace and tilted her chin upward with the curved fingers of his right hand. "I'm sorry," he said huskily.

Sharon forgave him, but not because of any nobility on her part. She couldn't help herself.

She stood on tiptoe, and her lips were just touching Tony's when the doorbell rang.

"One of the kids will get it," he assured her in a whisper, propelling her into a deep kiss when she would have drawn back.

The kiss left Sharon bedazzled and more than a little bewildered, and she was staring mutely up at Tony when Bri bounded into the room and announced, "There's a man here to see you, Mom. He says his name is Sven Svensen."

"Sven Svensen," Tony muttered with a shake of his head. His hands fell away from Sharon's waist and he retreated from her to roll up his blueprints and tuck them back into their cardboard tube.

Sven appeared in the doorway of the den only a second later, tall and blond and spectacular. He was indeed the Sven that Sharon remembered from high school, and his exuberance seemed to fill the room.

"All these years I have dreamed of you," he cried, spreading his hands. But then his eyes strayed to Tony. "This is your husband? This is the father of your children?"

"No to the first question," Sharon answered, keeping her distance, "and yes to the second. Tony and I are divorced."

Sven beamed after taking a moment to figure out the situation, and she introduced the two men to each other properly.

Tony's eyebrows rose when Sven grasped Sharon by the waist and thrust her toward the ceiling with a shout of joyous laughter. "Still you are so beautiful, just like when you were a leadcheerer!"

The altitude was getting to Sharon in a hurry. She smiled down at Sven. "You haven't changed much, either," she said lamely.

He lowered her back to the floor, his happy smile lighting up the whole room. Tony's expression provided an interesting contrast; he looked as though he was ready to clout somebody over the head with his cardboard tube of blueprints.

"What brings you back to America?" Sharon asked her unexpected guest, nervously smoothing her slacks with both hands.

"I am big businessman now," Sven answered expansively. "I travel all over the world."

Sharon was aware that Tony was leaving, but she pretended not to notice. If he felt a little jealous, so be it; she'd certainly done her share of agonizing over the mysterious Ingrid.

It was then that the idea occurred to Sharon.

"Will you be in the area for a while, Sven?" she asked, taking his arm. "There's this party on the night of the twenty-second—"

"You talk to him!" Michael raged, flinging his arms wide in exclamation as his father entered the small office trailer parked on the site of the new supermarket. "The man has a head of solid marble—there's no reasoning with him!"

Tony glared at his brother, but said nothing. The argument, beginning that morning, had been escalating all day.

Vincent met Tony's gaze for a moment, then looked at Michael. "I could hear the two of you 'reasoning' with each other on the other side of the lot. Exactly what is the problem?"

Tony was glad Michael launched into an answer first, because he didn't have one prepared. All he knew was that he felt like fighting.

"I'll tell you what the problem is," Michael began furiously, waggling an index finger at his elder brother. "Tony's got trouble with Sharon and he's been taking it out on me ever since he got here this morning!"

Michael's accusation was true, but Tony couldn't bring himself to admit it. He folded his arms and clamped his jaw down tight. He was still in the mood for an all-out brawl, and his brother seemed like a good candidate for an opponent.

Vincent gazed imploringly at the ceiling. "I am retired," he told some invisible entity. "Why don't I have the good sense to go to Florida and lie in the sun like other men my age?"

Tony's mind was wandering; he thought of that Sven character hoisting Sharon up in the air the way he had, and even though his collar was already loose, he felt a need to pull at it with his finger. He wondered if she found that kind of man attractive; some women liked foreign accents and caveman tactics....

"Tonio?" Michael snapped his fingers in front of his brother's eyes. "Do you think you can be a part of this conversation, or shall we just go on without you?"

Vincent chuckled. "Do not torment your brother, Michael," he said. "Can't you see that he's already miserable?"

Michael sighed, but his eyes were still hot with anger. "You were thinking about Sharon when you fell and damn near killed yourself, weren't you, Tony?" he challenged. After an awkward moment during which Tony remained stubbornly silent, he went on. "Now, you seem determined to alienate every craftsman within a fifty-mile radius. How the hell do you expect to bring this project in on time and within budget if we lose every worker we've got?"

Vincent cleared his throat. "Tonio," he said diplomatically, "I was supposed to be at home an hour ago. If I walk out of this trailer, what is my assurance that the two of you will be able to work through this thing without killing each other?"

Tony sighed. "Maybe I have been a little touchy lately—"

"A *little* touchy?" Michael demanded, shaking his finger again.

"Unless you want to eat it," Tony said, "you'd better stop waving that damned finger in my face!"

The sound of the dialing mechanism on the telephone broke the furious silence that followed. "Hello, Maria?" Vincent said. "This is the man who fathered your six children calling. If I come home now, I fear you will be left with only four.... Yes, yes, I will tell them. Goodbye, my love."

Michael shoved one hand through his hair as

his father hung up. "Tell us what?" he ventured to ask.

"Your mother says that her cousin Earnestine has been very happy as the mother of four children," Vincent answered, reaching for his hat. "My orders are to leave you to work out your differences as you see fit, whether you kill each other or not. Good night, my sons."

Tony and Michael grinned at each other when the door of the trailer closed behind their father.

"Come on," Michael said gruffly. "I'll buy you a beer and we'll talk about these personality problems of yours."

Tony had nothing better to do than go out for a beer, but he wondered about Michael. "Don't you have a date or something?"

His brother looked at his watch. "Ingrid will understand if I'm a little late," he answered. "She knows you've been having a tough time."

Tony was annoyed. His hands immediately went to his hips, and he was scowling. "Is there anybody in Port Webster you haven't regaled with the grisly saga of Tony Morelli?"

"Yes," Michael answered affably. "Sharon. If you won't tell the woman you're crazy about her, maybe I ought to."

"You do and a certain old lady will be lighting lots of candles in front of your picture,'' Tony responded with conviction.

Michael shrugged, and the two brothers left the trailer.

Helen's eyes sparkled and she lifted one hand to her mouth to stifle a giggle when Sharon described her visit from Sven Svensen the night before.

''And Tony was there when he arrived?'' she whispered in delighted scandal.

Sharon nodded. ''Sven has business in Seattle, but he'll be back here on the twenty-second to take me to the company party.''

Helen clapped her hands. ''Thank heaven Mrs. Morelli invited Allen and me,'' she crowed. ''I wouldn't want to miss this for anything! You'll wear that fantastic dress, of course.''

Again, Sharon nodded. But she was a little distracted. ''There is one thing I have to tell you about my trip to Paris,'' she began reluctantly.

Helen leaned forward, one perfectly shaped eyebrow arched in silent question.

''I can't go,'' Sharon confided with a grimace. ''Susan says I absolutely can't afford it.''

"Well, there's always next spring," Helen reasoned. "November isn't the greatest time—"

"That isn't the problem," Sharon broke in. "I told Tony all about the trip—I made it sound like a big deal. If I say I can't go because I don't have the money, he'll laugh at me."

"I can't imagine Tony doing that," Helen said solemnly.

"You haven't seen his financial statement," Sharon replied. "He pays more in taxes for a month than I make in six."

"He stepped right into a thriving business," Helen pointed out. "You started your own. Anyway, Morelli Construction is a partnership. Maybe Tony's had a big part in the company's success, but he can't take all the credit for it."

Sharon sighed. A woman was examining the items in the display window, but she didn't look as though she was going to come in and buy anything. It was time for the Christmas rush to begin, if only people would start rushing. "What would you do if you were me?"

Helen drew a deep breath. On the exhalation, she said, "I'd go straight to Tony and tell him that I loved him, and then I'd not only ask him to pay for the trip to Paris, I'd invite him along.

Whereupon he would accept graciously and I would kiss his knees in gratitude.''

''You're no help at all,'' Sharon said, giving Helen a look before she walked away to put each half-slip on a rack exactly one inch from the next one.

Sharon sat in front of the lighted mirror in her too-big, too-empty bedroom, carefully applying her makeup.

''I don't understand why you want to go out with that guy, anyway,'' Bri said, pouting. Curled up on the foot of the bed, she had been watching her stepmother get ready for the big party. ''He's not nearly as good-looking as Daddy.''

Sharon privately agreed, but she wasn't about to look a gift-Swede in the mouth. Her only other options, after all, were staying home from the party or going without an escort and spending a whole evening watching Tony attend to Ingrid. She shuddered.

''I knew you'd get cold in that dress,'' Matt observed from the doorway. ''I can practically see your belly button.''

Sharon gave her son an arch look. ''Did your father tell you to say that?'' she asked.

"He would if he saw the dress," Bri put in.

"Are you going to marry the Terminator?" Matt demanded to know.

After a smile at the nickname Sven didn't know he had, Sharon tilted her head back and raised one hand dramatically to her brow. "No, no, a thousand times no!" she cried.

"I think she should marry Daddy," Bri commented from her perch on the end of the bed.

Sharon was finished with her makeup and had now turned her attention to her hair. She let her stepdaughter's remark pass unchallenged.

"You could take him to Paris with you," Matt suggested. "Dad, I mean. You guys might decide you like each other and want to get married again."

"Paris is a city for lovers," Briana agreed with rising enthusiasm.

"Your dad and I are not lovers." Sharon felt a twinge of guilt, which she hid by reaching for her brush and sweeping her hair up into a small knot at the back of her head. She hadn't been able to tell the kids that the Paris trip was off, mostly because she knew they would go straight to Tony with the news. It would be too humiliating to have him know that she was having a hard time financially while he was making a success of everything he did.

Her plan was to hide out on the island for a few days and let everyone think that she was in Paris. She didn't look forward to living a lie, but for now, at least, she couldn't bear for Tony to think that she was anything less than a glittering sensation.

"I don't understand why no kids are allowed at this party," Bri complained, biting her lower lip. "It would be fun to wear something shiny."

"To match your grillwork," Matt teased.

Sharon was relieved that the conversation had taken a twist in another direction, away from Paris and lovers and Tony. "Don't start fighting now, you guys. Scary Harry will want double wages for watching you."

Bri had folded her arms and was studiously ignoring her brother. The combined gesture was reminiscent of Tony. "Gramma and Grampa include us kids in everything else," she said. "Why is this party for adults only?"

"You said it yourself," Sharon answered, turning her head from side to side so that she could make sure her hair looked good before spraying it. "Your grandparents include you and your nine hundred cousins in everything else.

There has to be one occasion that's just for grown-ups.''

"Why?" Bri immediately retorted. "There isn't one that's just for kids."

The doorbell chimed, and Sharon was grateful. "Go and answer that, please," she said, reaching out for her favorite cologne and giving herself a generous misting.

"It's probably the Terminator," Matt grumbled, but Bri dashed out of the bedroom and down the stairs to answer the door.

Five minutes later Sharon descended the staircase in her glittering red dress to greet a tall and handsome man wearing a tuxedo. Everything would have been perfect if the man had been Tony and not Sven.

The Swede had not been exaggerating when he had described himself as a "big business-man," physical stature aside. Sven was obviously successful; he'd proved it by arriving in a chauffeured limousine.

Sharon's eyes were wide as she settled herself in the suede-upholstered back seat and looked around.

"You like this, no?" Sven asked, with the eagerness of a child displaying a favorite toy.

"I like this, yes," Sharon answered. "I'm impressed. You've done very well for yourself, Sven.''

Sven beamed. ''You too are doing well with your store selling underwear.''

Sharon laughed and squeezed his hand. ''Oh, Sven,'' she said. ''You do have a way with words.''

''This will be a very interesting evening, I think,'' Sven replied, his pale eyebrows moving up. ''This old husband of yours, the one you do not anymore want—tell me about him.''

Sharon sighed, and then related a great many ordinary things about Tony. There must have been something revealing in her tone or her manner, because Sven took her hand and sympathetically patted it with his own as the sleek limo sped toward the first event of the holiday season.

10

The banquet room of Port Webster's yacht club shimmered with silvery lights. Even though there were hordes of people, Sharon's gaze locked with Tony's the moment she and Sven walked through the door.

Her heart fishtailed like a car on slick pavement, then righted itself. Tony looked fabulous in his tuxedo, and the woman standing at his side was tall and lithe with blond hair that tumbled like a waterfall to her waist.

Ingrid, no doubt.

Glumly, Sharon resigned herself to being short and perky. *Cute*, God forbid. In high school those attributes had stood her in good stead; in the here and now they seemed absolutely insipid.

"Someone has died?" Sven inquired, with a teasing light in his blue eyes as he bent to look into Sharon's crestfallen face. "The stock market has crashed?"

Sharon forced herself to smile, and it was a good thing because Tony was making his way toward them, pulling Ingrid along with him.

A waiter arrived at the same moment, and Sven graciously accepted glasses of champagne for himself and his nervous date. Sharon practically did a swan dive into her drink.

Sven stepped gallantly into the conversational breach. "So, we meet again," he said to Tony, but his eyes were on Ingrid.

Tony's jawline clamped down, then relaxed. Ingrid had slipped her arm through his and clasped her hands together.

Sharon wondered why the woman didn't just execute a half nelson and be done with it, but she would have eaten one of the centerpieces before letting either Tony or Ingrid know how ill at ease she felt.

"Are you Sharon?" the blonde demanded pleasantly, extending one hand in greeting before Tony could introduce her. "I've been so eager to meet you!"

I'll just bet you have, Sharon thought sourly, but she kept right on looking cute and perky.

"Yes," she answered, "and I presume you're Ingrid?"

The blonde nodded. She really was stunning, and her simple, black cocktail dress did a lot to show off her long, shapely legs. She seemed genuinely pleased to know Sharon, though her gaze had, by this time, strayed to Sven. "Hello," she said in her throaty voice.

Sharon took a hasty sip of her champagne and spilled a little of it when Tony took hold of her elbow, without warning, and pulled her aside. "If I stick that guy with a pin, will he deflate and fly around the room?" he asked, feigning a serious tone.

Sharon glared at her ex-husband. "If you stick Sven with a pin, I imagine he'll punch you in the mouth," she responded.

Tony looked contemptuously unterrified. He lifted his champagne glass to his mouth, taking a sip as his eyes moved over Sharon's dress. "Where did you buy that—Dolly Parton's last garage sale?"

Sharon refrained from stomping on his instep only because Sven and Ingrid were present. "You don't like it?" she countered sweetly, batting her lashes. "Good."

"We are from the same town in Sweden, Ingrid and I!'' Sven exclaimed in that buoyant way of his.

''Would you mind if I borrowed your date for just one dance?'' Ingrid asked Sharon. She didn't seem to care what Tony's opinion might be.

''Be my guest,'' Sharon said magnanimously.

''Michael is going to love this,'' Tony muttered, as he watched Sven and Ingrid walk away.

Sharon was desperate for a safe topic of conversation, and her former brother-in-law was it. She craned her neck, looking for him. ''I'd enjoy a waltz with Michael,'' she said. ''He's the best dancer in the family.''

Tony took Sharon's glass out of her hand and set it on a table with his own. ''You'll have to settle for me, because my brother isn't here,'' he said. His fingers closed over hers and she let him lead her toward the crowded dance floor.

To distract herself from the sensations dancing with Tony aroused in various parts of her anatomy, Sharon looked up at him and asked, ''Michael, missing a party? I don't believe it.''

''Believe it. He's out of town, putting in a bid on a new mall.''

Sharon lifted her eyebrows. ''Impressive.''

''It will make ours the biggest construction

operation in this part of the state,'' Tony replied without any particular enthusiasm.

Sharon thought of her canceled trip to Paris and sighed. ''I guess some of us have it and some of us don't,'' she said softly.

Tony's hand caught under her chin. ''What was that supposed to mean?'' he asked. His voice was gentle, the look in his eyes receptive.

Sharon nearly told him the truth, but lost her courage at the last millisecond. She couldn't risk opening herself up to an I-told-you-so or, worse yet, a generous helping of indulgent sympathy. ''Nothing,'' she said, forcing a bright smile to her face.

There was a flicker of disappointment in Tony's eyes. ''Is it that hard to talk to me?'' he asked quietly.

Sharon let the question go unanswered, pretending that she hadn't heard it, and turned her head to watch Sven and Ingrid for a moment. ''There's something so damned cheerful about them,'' she muttered.

Tony chuckled, but there was scant amusement in the sound. Maybe, Sharon reflected with a pang, he was jealous of Ingrid's obvious rapport with Sven. When she looked up into those familiar brown eyes, they were solemn.

Resolved to get through this night with her dignity intact if it killed her, Sharon smiled up at him. "I'm surprised I haven't met Ingrid before this," she said brightly.

Tony shrugged. "If you'd come to any of the family gatherings lately, you would have," he observed, as though it were the most natural thing in the world for a woman to socialize with her ex-husband's girlfriend.

Sharon was inexpressibly wounded to know that Tony cared enough about Ingrid to include her in the mob scenes that were a way of life in the Morelli family. Reminding herself that she and Tony were no longer husband and wife, that she had no real part in his life anymore, did nothing to ease the pain.

The plain and simple truth was that she had been replaced with the simple ease and aplomb she'd always feared she would be. Her smile wavered.

"I've been busy lately," she said, and then, mercifully, the music stopped and Sven and Ingrid were at hand. Sharon pulled free of Tony's embrace and turned blindly into Sven's. "Dance with me," she whispered in desperate tones, as the small orchestra began another waltz.

Sven's expression was full of tenderness and

concern. "So much you love this man that your heart is breaking," he said. "Poor little bird—I cannot bear to see you this way."

Sharon let her forehead rest against her friend's strong shoulder, struggling to maintain her composure. It would be disastrous to fall apart in front of all these people. "I'll be fine," she told him, but the words sounded uncertain.

"We will leave this place," Sven responded firmly. "It is not good for you, being here."

Sharon drew a deep breath and let it out again. She couldn't leave, not yet. She wouldn't let the pain of loving and losing Tony bring her to her knees that way. She lifted her chin and, with a slight shake of her head, said, "No. I'm not going to run away."

An expression of gentle respect flickered in Sven's blue eyes. "We will make the best of this situation, then," he said. He looked like the shy, awkward teenager Sharon had known in high school when he went on. "There are other men who want you, little bird," he told her. "I am one of these."

Gently, Sharon touched Sven's handsome, freshly shaven face. A sweet, achy sense of remorse filled her. He'd been so kind to her; she didn't want to hurt him. She started to speak, but Sven silenced her by laying one index finger to her lips.

"Don't speak," he said. "I know you are not ready to let a new man love you. Do you want him back, Sharon—this Tony of yours?"

"I've asked myself that question a million times," Sharon confided. "The truth is, I do, but I know it can never work."

"He betrayed you? He was with other women?"

Sharon shook her head.

"He drank?" Sven persisted, frowning. "He beat you?"

Sharon laughed. Tony liked good wine, but she'd never actually seen him drunk in all the years she'd known him, although there had been that incident Michael had mentioned weeks before. Tony had always been a lover, not a fighter. "No," she answered.

"Then why are you divorced from him?" Sven asked, looking genuinely puzzled.

"There are other reasons for divorce," Sharon replied, as the orchestra paused between numbers.

"Like what?" Sven wanted to know, as he led Sharon off the dance floor. He'd seated her at a table and secured drinks for them both before she answered.

For some reason—perhaps it was the champagne—Sharon found that she could talk to Sven, and the words came pouring out of her. "Tony was married once before when he was very young. His wife was killed in a terrible accident, and he was left with a baby girl to raise. He and I met only a few months after Carmen died."

Sven took her hand. "And?" he prompted.

"I know people say this doesn't happen to real people, but the moment I saw Tony I fell in love with him."

Sven smiled sadly, and his grasp on Sharon's fingers tightened a little. "Tell me how you met your Tony."

Sharon sighed. "I was working in a bookstore here in Port Webster and going to business college at night." She paused, gazing back into the past. "He made his selections, and I was one of them, I guess. We went out that night, and six weeks later we were married."

"You say that as though you were one of the books he bought," Sven observed. "Why is this?"

Sharon shrugged, but her expression was one

of quiet sorrow. "There have been times when I felt that he'd chosen me for a purpose, the same way he chose those books. He was lonely, and he needed a mother for his daughter."

"Children can be raised successfully without a mother," Sven put in.

Sharon nodded. "That's true, of course," she conceded. "And heaven knows there are enough kids growing up without a father. But Tony is—well—he's family oriented. It's the most important thing in the world to him." She swallowed. He'd remarried quickly after Carmen, and he was going to do the same thing now. Exit wife number two, enter number three.

"You're going to cry, I think," Sven said. "We can't have that, since he's looking our way, your buyer of books." Rising from his chair, the Swede drew Sharon out of hers, as well. "Trust me when I do this, little bird," he said huskily, and then, with no more warning than that, he swept Sharon into his arms and gave her a kiss that left her feeling as though she'd had her head held under water for five minutes.

She blushed hotly, one hand to her breast, and hissed, "Sven!"

His azure eyes twinkled as he looked down at

her. "Now we can leave," he said. "We have given your used-to-be lover something to think about on this cold winter night."

It seemed unlikely that Tony would spend the night thinking—not when he'd have Ingrid lying in bed beside him—but Sharon knew that Sven was right about one thing. She could escape that ghastly party now without looking like the scorned ex-wife.

She felt Tony's gaze touching her as she waited for Sven to return with her coat, but she refused to meet it. It was time to cut her losses.

After saying a few words to Vincent and Maria, and to Helen and her husband, Allen, Sharon left the party with her hand in the crook of Sven's powerful arm and her chin held high. The plush interior of the limousine was warm and welcoming.

"You will come to my suite for drinks and more talk of old times, no?" Sven asked.

"No," Sharon confirmed.

Her friend frowned. "You must," he said.

Sharon squirmed a little. Maybe Sven wasn't as understanding as she'd thought. "If I have to jump for it," she warned, "I will."

Sven laughed. "I am more the gentleman than this, little bird. And since I am a man, I know how your Tony is thinking now. He will either telephone or drive past your house at the first opportunity. Do you want to be there, sipping hot cocoa and knitting by the fireside? Of course you don't!''

Sven's theory had its merits, but Sharon wasn't ready for an intimate relationship with a new man, and she had to be sure that her friend understood that. "Promise you won't get me into another lip-lock?" she asked seriously.

Sven gave a shout of amusement. "What is this 'lip-lock'?" he countered.

"I was referring to that kiss back at the party," Sharon said, her arms folded. "Nobody under seventeen should have been allowed to see that unless they were accompanied by a parent."

Sven's eyes, blue as a fjord under a clear sky, danced with mischief. "I wish you could have seen Tony's face, little bird," he said. "You would feel better if you had."

Sharon bit her lip. It seemed just as likely to her that Sven's trick would backfire and propel Tony into some R-rated adventures of his own, but she didn't want to spoil her friend's delight by saying so. "I don't want to talk about Tony anymore," she said. "Tell me about you, Sven."

Since there was no hotel in Port Webster, the limo rolled toward nearby Tacoma, where Sven's company had provided him with a suite. During the drive he told Sharon about his company, which manufactured ski equipment that would soon be sold in the United States. He also mentioned his short and disastrous marriage, which had ended two years before.

As Sven was helping Sharon out of the limo in front of his hotel, she stepped on the hem of her slinky dress and felt the slit move a few inches higher on her thigh. "Oh, great," she muttered.

Sven chuckled. "There is a problem, no?"

"There is a problem, yes, I've torn my dress," Sharon answered. "And I'm not getting the hang of this being single, Sven. I'm not adjusting."

His hand was strong on the small of her back as he ushered her toward the warmth and light of the lobby. "It takes time," he told her. "Much time and not a little pain."

Sharon was glad she was wearing a long coat when they stepped inside that elegant hotel. There were a lot of people milling around, and she didn't want them to see that the sexy slit in her dress had been extended to the area of her tonsils.

"You are hungry?" Sven asked, as they passed a dark restaurant looking out over Commencement Bay.

Except for a few hors d'oeuvres, Sharon had had nothing to eat all evening, and all that champagne was just sloshing around in her stomach, waiting to cause trouble. "I suppose I am," she confessed, "but I don't want to take off my coat."

Sven chuckled. "Little bird, there is only candlelight in there. Who will see that your dress is torn?"

Sharon succumbed to his logic, partly because she'd missed supper and partly because she wanted to delay for as long as possible the moment when she and Sven stepped inside his suite. She loved Tony Morelli with all her heart and soul, but her desires hadn't died with their divorce. Sven's kiss, back at the party, had proved that much to her.

They enjoyed a leisurely dinner, during which they laughed and talked and drank a great deal of champagne. By the time they got to Sven's suite, Sharon's mind was foggy, and she was yawning like a sleepy child.

Sven gave her an innocuous kiss and said, "How I wish that I were the kind of man to take advantage of you, little bird. Just for tonight, I would like to be such a scoundrel."

Sharon sighed and smiled a tipsy smile. By then she was carrying her shoes in one hand and her hair was falling down from its pins. "Know what?" she asked. "I wish I could be different, too. Here I am in a fancy suite with a man who should be featured in one of those hunk-of-the-month calendars, and what do I do with such an opportunity? I waste it, that's what."

Sven grinned, cupping her face with his large, gentle hands. "Always, since I was here for high school, when I think of America, I think of you," he said with a sigh of his own. "Ah, Sharon, Sharon—the way you looked in those jeans of yours made me want to defect and ask for political asylum in this country."

Sharon stood on tiptoe to kiss his cheek. "Nobody defects from Sweden," she reasoned.

Sven put her away with a gentle purposefulness that said a lot about his sense of honor, and looked down at his slender gold watch. "It is time, I believe, to take you home," he said in a gruff voice. "It would seem that my wish to become a scoundrel is beginning to come true."

"Oh." Sharon swallowed and retreated a step. She had removed her coat in the restaurant, but she'd put it on again before they left. Now she held it a little closer around her.

"When next I come to America," Sven went on, his back to Sharon now as he looked out at the bay and the lights that adorned it like diamonds upon velvet, "you may be through loving Tony. For obvious reasons, I want you to remember me kindly if that is the case."

Sharon had had a great deal to drink that evening, but she was sober enough to appreciate Sven's gallantry. "You don't have to worry about that," she said softly. "My having kind thoughts about you, I mean. I'm no sophisticate, but I know that men like you are rare."

When Sven turned to face her, he was once again flashing that dazzling smile of his. It was as reassuring as a beam from a lighthouse on a dark and storm-tossed sea. "What you have yet to learn, little bird," he told her, "is that you also are special. You are fireworks and blue jeans and county fairs—everything that is American."

Sharon shrugged, feeling sheepish and rumpled and very safe. "I'm going to take that as a compliment since I've had too much booze to fight back if it was an insult,'' she said.

Sven laughed again and went to the telephone to summon the limousine and driver his company had provided for him.

It was 3:00 a.m. exactly when the limo came to a stop in front of the house on Tamarack Drive, and Tony's car was parked in the driveway.

Sven smiled mysteriously, as though some private theory of his had been proven correct. "You would like me to come in with you?" he inquired.

He didn't look surprised when Sharon shook her head. She knew she had nothing to fear from Tony, even if he was in a raving fury, but she wasn't so sure that the same was true of Sven. With her luck the two men would get into a brawl, half kill each other and scar the kids' psyches for life.

"Thanks for everything," she said, reaching for the knob. As she'd expected, the door was unlocked. "And good night."

Sven gave her a brotherly kiss on the forehead and then walked away.

The light was on in the entryway, and there was a lamp burning in the living room. Barefoot, her strappy silver shoes dangling from one hand, Sharon followed the trail Tony had left for her.

He was in the den, lying on the sofa bed and watching the shopping channel. He was wearing battered jeans and a T-shirt, and his feet were bare. He didn't look away when Sharon came to stand beside the bed.

She glanced at the TV screen. A hideously ornate clock with matching candelabras was being offered for roughly the price an oil sheikh's firstborn son would bring on the black market. "Thinking of redecorating?"

Tony sighed, still staring at the screen. "Who do I look like?" he countered. "Herman Munster?"

Sharon tossed her shoes aside and sat down on the edge of the mattress. "What are you doing here?" she asked.

He rubbed his chin with one hand. "I seem to have some kind of homing device implanted in my brain. Every once in a while I forget that I don't live here anymore."

Sharon felt sad and broken. The slit in the dress she hadn't been able to afford went higher with an audible rip when she curled her legs beneath her. She plucked at the blanket with two fingers and kept her eyes down. "Oh," she said.

Tony's voice was like gravel. "Do you know what time it is?" he demanded.

Sharon's sadness was displaced by quiet outrage. "Yes," she answered. "It's 3:05, the party's over and a good time was had by all. You can leave anytime now, Tony."

He reached out with such quick ferocity that Sharon's eyes went wide, and he caught her wrist in one hand. Even though Tony wasn't hurting her, Sharon felt her heart trip into a faster, harder beat, and her breath was trapped in her lungs.

Before she knew what was happening, she was lying on her back, looking up into his face. A muscle flexed along his jawline. He was resting part of his weight on her, and even though she was angry, Sharon welcomed it.

"If you're in love with that Swede," Tony said evenly, "I want to know it. Right now."

Sharon swallowed. "I'm not really sober enough to handle this," she said.

Tony looked as though he might be torn between kissing Sharon and killing her. "Fine. If I have to pour coffee down your throat all night long, I'll do it."

She squeezed her eyes shut. "I really think you should let me go," she said.

"Give me one good reason," Tony replied.

"I'm going to throw up."

He rolled aside. "That's a good reason if I've ever heard one," he conceded, as Sharon leaped off the bed, a hand clasped to her mouth, and ran for the adjoining bathroom.

When she came out some minutes later, Tony was waiting with her favorite chenille bathrobe draped over one arm, and a glass of bicarbonate in his hand.

Sharon drank the seltzer down in a series of gulps and then let Tony divest her of the coat. He did raise an eyebrow when he saw that the slit had advanced to well past her hip, but to his credit he made no comment. He turned her so that he could unzip the dress, and Sharon didn't protest.

Her hair was a mess, her mascara was running and her gown—which she would still be paying for in six months—was totally ruined. She couldn't afford her trip to Paris, and she loved a man she couldn't live with.

It was getting harder and harder to take a positive outlook on things.

11

The hangover was there to meet Sharon when she woke up in the morning. Head throbbing, stomach threatening revolt, she groaned and buried her face deep in her pillow when she heard Tony telling the kids to keep the noise down.

Sharon lifted her head slightly and opened one eye. She was in the den.

There was a cheerful blaze snapping and crackling in the fireplace, and Matt was perched on the foot of the hide-a-bed, watching Saturday morning cartoons. Tony was working at the desk, while Briana strutted back and forth with Sharon's ruined dress draped against her front.

"That must have been some party," the child observed, inspecting the ripped seam.

"Coffee," Sharon moaned. "If anyone in this room has a shred of decency in their soul, they'll bring me some right now."

Tony chuckled and got out of his chair. Moments later he was back with a mug of steaming coffee, and the kids had mysteriously vanished. "Here you go, you party animal," he said, as Sharon scrambled to an upright position and reached out for the cup with two trembling hands.

"Thanks," she grumbled.

Tony sat on the edge of the bed. "Want some breakfast?"

"There is no need to be vicious," Sharon muttered. The coffee tasted good, but two sips told her the stuff wasn't welcome in her stomach.

He laughed and kissed her forehead. "You'll feel better later," he said gently. "I promise."

She set the coffee aside and shoved a hand through her rumpled hair. "You're being awfully nice to me," she said suspiciously, squinting at the clock on the mantelpiece. "What time is it, anyway?"

Tony sighed. "It's time you were up and getting ready for your trip to Paris. Your flight leaves Seattle this afternoon, doesn't it?"

Sharon settled herself against the back of the sofa and groaned. She wanted so much to confess that she was really planning to spend the next four days on the island, but she couldn't. She had an image to maintain. "Yes," she said.

"I'd like to drive you to the airport," Tony told her.

Sharon stared at him. Although she wanted to accept, she couldn't because then, of course, Tony would find out that she wasn't really going anywhere. "That won't be necessary," she replied, dropping her eyes.

Never a man to let well enough alone, Tony persisted. "Why not?"

Sharon was trapped. She could either lie or admit that she was a failure and a fraud. She gnawed at her lower lip for a moment and then blurted out, "Because Sven is seeing me off."

There was a short, deadly silence, then Tony stood. "Great," he said, moving toward the desk, gathering whatever he'd been working on earlier.

Sharon steeled herself against an impulse to offer him frantic assurances that she and Sven weren't involved. After all, Tony wasn't letting any grass grow under his feet, romantically speaking. He had Ingrid. "I knew you'd understand," she hedged, reaching for her chenille bathrobe and hopping out of bed. She was tying the belt when Tony finally turned around to face her again.

"I don't have the right to ask you this," he said, his voice gruff and barely audible over the sounds of muted cartoons and the fire on the hearth. "But I've got to know. Is he—Sven—going to Paris with you?"

Sharon's throat ached with suppressed emotion; she knew what it had cost Tony, in terms of his dignity, to ask that question. She could only shake her head.

Tony nodded, his eyes revealing a misery Sharon didn't know how to assuage, and said, "I'll just take the kids out for a while, if that's okay. Have a good trip."

The guilt Sharon felt was monumental. She loved these people, Tony and Briana and Matt, and she was lying to them, acting out an elaborate charade for the sake of her pride.

"I will," she said. "Thanks."

He gave her a look of wry anguish. "Sure," he answered, and within five minutes Briana and Matt had said goodbye to Sharon and left with Tony.

Woodenly, Sharon trudged upstairs, got out of her robe and the nightgown she had no memory of putting on, and stepped into a hot shower.

When she came out, she felt better physically, but her emotions were as tangled as yarn mauled by a kitten.

She put on jeans and a burgundy cable-knit sweater, along with heavy socks and hiking boots. "Just the outfit for jetting off to Paris," she muttered, slumping down on the side of the bed and reaching for the telephone.

Helen answered on the second ring. "Teddy Bares. May I help you?"

Sharon sighed. "I wish someone could. How's business this morning?"

"We're doing pretty well," Helen replied. "Everything is under control. That was some kiss old Sven laid on you at the party last night, my dear."

"I was hoping no one noticed," Sharon said lamely.

"You must know that Tony did. He left five minutes after you and Sven went out the door, and your former in-laws had to take the blonde home because he forgot her."

Sharon's spirits rose a little at the thought of Ingrid slipping Tony's mind like that. She said nothing, sensing that Helen would carry the conversational ball.

"If I ever had any doubt that Tony Morelli is

nuts about you, and only you, it's gone now."
She paused to draw a deep, philosophical breath.
"You're not still going through with this trip-
to-Paris thing, are you?"

"I have to," Sharon said, rubbing her temple
with three fingers.

"Nonsense."

Sharon didn't have the energy to argue. The
shop had been a big part of the reason she and
Tony had gotten divorced; he was very old-
fashioned in a lot of ways, and she doubted that
he understood even now why she wanted the
hassles of owning a business. If she didn't suc-
ceed, all his misgivings would be justified. "I'll
be back the day before Thanksgiving," she said
firmly. "If there are any emergencies in the
meantime, you know where to call."

Helen sighed. "This is never going to work,
you know. The truth will come out."

"Maybe so," Sharon replied, "but it had better not come out of you, my friend. I'll explain
this to Tony myself—someday."

"Right," Helen said crisply. "Tell me this—
what number are you going to give him to call
if one of the kids gets sick or something? He'll
expect you to be registered in a hotel...."

"I told Tony several days ago that I'd be

checking in with you regularly, so if anything goes wrong, you'll hear from him. All you would have to do then is call me at the A-frame.''

''This is stupid, Sharon.''

''I don't recall asking for your opinion,'' Sharon retorted.

''What about postcards?'' Helen shot back. ''What about souvenirs for the kids? Don't you see that you're not going to be able to pull this off?''

Sharon bit her lip. The deception was indeed a tangled web, and it was getting stickier by the moment, but she was already trapped. ''I'll check out that import shop in Seattle or something,'' she said.

''You're crazy,'' commented Helen.

''It's nice to know that my friends are solidly behind me,'' Sharon snapped.

There was a pause, and then Helen said quietly, ''I want you to be happy. You do know that, don't you?''

''Yes,'' Sharon replied distractedly. ''Goodbye, Helen. I'll see you when I get back from— Paris.''

''Right.'' Helen sighed, and the conversation was over.

Sharon packed jeans, warm sweaters and flannel nightgowns for the trip, leaving behind the trim suits and dresses she would have taken to Europe. Such things would, of course, be of no use on the island.

She loaded her suitcase into the trunk of her roadster and set out for Seattle and the import shop she had in mind. First things first, she reflected dismally, as she sped along the freeway.

Halfway there, she asked herself, "What am I doing?" right out loud and took the next exit. Within minutes, she was headed back toward Port Webster.

Enough was enough. Surely going through all this was more demeaning than admitting the truth to Tony could ever be.

Sharon drove by his condominium first, but no one answered the door. With a sigh, she got back into the roadster and set out for his parents' house. Reaching that, Sharon almost lost her courage. There were cars everywhere; obviously something was going on. Something big.

Resigned, Sharon found a place for her roadster, got out and walked toward the enormous, noisy house. The very structure seemed to be permeated with love and laughter, and she smiled sadly as she reached out to ring the doorbell. She didn't belong here anymore; maybe she never had.

Vincent opened the door, and his look of delight enveloped Sharon like a warm blanket and drew her in out of the biting November cold. "Come in, come in," he said, taking her hand in his strong grasp. "We're having a celebration."

Sharon lingered in the entryway when Vincent would have led her into the living room. "A celebration?" she echoed.

Vincent spread his hands and beamed in triumph. "At last, he is getting married, my stubborn son...."

Sharon's first reaction was primitive and instantaneous; her stomach did a flip, and she wanted to turn and flee like a frightened rabbit. A deep breath, however, marked the return of rational thought. Maybe things weren't very good between her and Tony, and maybe they weren't communicating like grown-up people were supposed to do, but she knew he wouldn't get married again without telling her. A man would think to mention something that important.

"Come in and have some wine with us," Vincent said gently. He'd noticed Sharon's nervous manner, but he was far too polite to comment.

She shook her head. "If I could just talk to Tony for a few minutes..."

Vincent shrugged and disappeared, leaving Sharon to stand in the colorful glow of a stained-glass skylight, her hands clasped together.

Tony appeared within seconds, slid his gaze over Sharon's casual clothes and said in a low, bewildered tone, "Hi."

Sharon drew a deep breath, let it out and took the plunge. "I have to talk to you," she said, and she was surprised to feel the sting of tears in her eyes because she hadn't planned to cry.

He took her hand and led her to the foot of the stairway, where they sat down together on the second step. Tony's thumb moved soothingly over her fingers. "I'm listening, babe," he said gently.

With the back of her free hand, Sharon tried to dry her eyes. "I lied," she confessed, the words a blurted whisper. "I'm not going to Paris because I can't afford to—Teddy Bares isn't doing that well."

Tony sighed, and enclosing her hand between both of his, lifted it to his lips. He wasn't looking at her, but at the patch of jeweled sunshine cast onto the oaken floor of the entryway beneath the skylight. "Why did you feel you had to lie?" he asked after a very long time.

Sharon sniffled. "I was ashamed, that's why. I thought you'd laugh if you found out that I couldn't spare the money for a plane ticket."

"Laugh?" The word sounded hollow and raw, and the look in Tony's eyes revealed that she'd hurt him. "You expected me to laugh because you'd been disappointed? My God, Sharon, do you think I'm that much of a bastard?"

Sharon was taken aback by the intensity of Tony's pain; he looked and sounded as though he'd been struck. "I'm sorry," she whispered.

"Hell, that makes all the difference," Tony rasped in a furious undertone, releasing her hand with a suddenness that bordered on violence. "Damn it, you don't even know me, do you? We were married for ten years, and you have no idea who I am."

Sharon needed to reach Tony, to reassure him. "That's not true," she said, stricken.

"It is," he replied, his voice cold and distant as he stood up. "And I sure as hell don't know you."

Grasping the banister beside her, Sharon

pulled herself to her feet. "Tony, please listen to me—"

"If you'll excuse me," he interrupted with icy formality, "I have a brother who's celebrating his engagement." He paused and thrust one hand through his hair, and when he looked at Sharon, his eyes were hot with hurt and anger. "I hope to God Michael and Ingrid will do better than we did," he said.

Michael and Ingrid. Michael and Ingrid. The words were like a fist to the stomach for Sharon. She closed her eyes against the impact and hugged herself to keep from flying apart. "Can—can you keep the kids—the way we'd planned?" she managed to ask.

Tony was silent for so long that Sharon was sure he'd left her standing there in the entryway with her eyes squeezed shut and her arms wrapped around her middle, but he finally answered raggedly, "Sure. What do you want me to tell them?"

"That I love them," Sharon said, and then she turned blindly and groped for the doorknob. A larger, stronger hand closed over hers, staying her escape.

"You're in no condition to drive," Tony said flatly, and there wasn't a shred of emotion in his voice. "You're not going anywhere until you pull yourself together."

Sharon couldn't face him. She knew he was right, though; it would be irresponsible to drive in that emotional state. She let her forehead rest against the door, struggling to hold in sobs of sheer heartbreak.

Tentatively, he touched her shoulder. "Sharon," he said, and the name reverberated with hopelessness and grief.

She trembled with the effort to control her runaway feelings, and after a few more moments she had regained her composure. "I'll be on the island if the kids need me," she said.

"Okay," Tony whispered, and he stepped back, allowing her to open the door and walk out.

Sharon drove to the ferry landing and boarded the boat. She didn't get out of the car and go up to the snack bar to drink coffee and look at the view, though. She wasn't interested in scenery.

Once the ferry docked, Sharon's brain began to work again. She set her course for the nearest supermarket and wheeled a cart up and down the aisles, selecting food with all the awareness of a robot.

The A-frame was cold since no one had been there in a while, and Sharon turned up the heat before she began putting her groceries away. Her soul was as numb as her body, but for a different reason.

The warmth wafting up from the vents in the floor would eventually take the chill of a November afternoon from her bones and muscles, but there was no remedy for the wintry ache in her spirit. She went into the living room and collapsed facedown on the sofa. She needed the release weeping would provide, but it eluded her. Evidently, she'd exhausted her supply of tears in the entryway of Vincent and Maria's house.

"How did it all go so wrong?" she asked, turning onto her back and gazing up at the ceiling with dry, swollen eyes.

The telephone jangled at just that moment, a shrill mockery in the silence. Sharon didn't want to answer, but she didn't have much choice. She had two children, and if they needed her, she had to know about it.

She crossed the room, indulged in a deep sniffle and spoke into the receiver in the most normal voice she was able to manage. "Hello?"

"Are you all right?" Tony wanted to know.

Sharon wound her finger in the phone cord. "I'm terrific," she replied. "Just terrific. Is anything wrong?"

"The kids are fine." The words immediately put Sharon's mind at rest.

"Good. Then you won't mind if I hang up. Goodbye, Tony, and enjoy the party."

"Except for that night when we were supposed to paint your apartment and ended up making love instead, I haven't enjoyed anything in eight months," Tony responded. "And don't you dare hang up."

Sharon drew a chair back from the nearby dining table and sank into it. "What am I supposed to say now, Tony? You tell me. That way, maybe I won't step on your toes and you won't step on mine and we can skip the usual fifteen rounds."

When Tony answered, that frosty distance was back in his voice. "Right now I feel like putting both my fists through the nearest wall. How can I be expected to know what either of us is supposed to say?"

"I guess you can't," Sharon replied. "And neither can I. Goodbye, Tony, and give my best to Michael and Ingrid."

"I will," Tony replied sadly, and then he hung up.

Sharon felt as though her whole body and spirit were one giant exposed nerve, throbbing in the cold. She replaced the receiver and went out for a long walk on the beach.

It was nearly dark when she returned to brew herself a cup of instant coffee, slide a frozen dinner into the oven and build a fire in the living room fireplace.

The flames seemed puny, and their warmth couldn't penetrate the chill that lingered around Sharon. She was eating her supper when the telephone rang again.

Again, she was forced to answer.

"Mom?" piped a voice on the other end of the line. "This is Matt."

Sharon smiled for the first time in hours. "I know. How are you, sweetheart?"

"I'm okay." Despite those words, Matt sounded worried. "Bri and I are spending the night with Gramma and Grampa. How come you didn't go to Paris like you said you were going to?"

Sharon clasped the bridge of her nose between her thumb and index finger. "I'll explain about

Paris when I get home, honey. Why aren't you and Bri sleeping at your dad's place?''

Before Matt could answer that, Bri joined the conversation on an extension. ''Something's really wrong,'' she said despairingly. ''You and Daddy are both acting very weird.''

Much as Sharon would have liked to refute that remark, she couldn't. ''I guess we are,'' she admitted softly. ''But everything is going to be all right again soon. I promise you that.''

She could feel Bri's confusion. ''Really?'' the girl asked in a small voice, and Sharon wished that she could put her arms around both her children and hold them close.

''Really,'' Sharon confirmed gently.

There was a quiet exchange on the other end of the line, and then Maria came on. ''Sharon? Are you all right, dear?''

Sharon swallowed. ''I guess so. Maria, why did Tony leave the children with you and Vincent? I understood him to say that he was going to look after them himself until I got back.''

Maria hesitated before answering. ''Tonio was upset when he left here,'' she said cautiously. ''Vincent was worried and went after him. I haven't seen either of them since.''

Sharon ached. Vincent Morelli was not the

kind of father who interfered in his children's lives; if he'd been worried enough to follow Tony, there was real cause for concern.

"Did Tony say anything before he left?"

Sharon realized that Maria was weeping softly. "No," the older woman answered. "I'd feel better if he had. He was just—just hurting."

"I see," Sharon said, keeping her chin high even though there was no one around to know that she was being brave.

"Tonio can be unkind when he is in pain," Maria ventured to say after a few moments of silence. It was obvious that she'd used the interval to work up her courage. "But he loves you, Sharon. He loves you very much."

Sharon nodded. "I love him, too—but sometimes that grand emotion just isn't enough."

"It's the greatest force in the world," Maria countered firmly. "You and Tonio don't understand how it works, that's all."

Sharon was still mulling that over when Maria changed the subject. "You'll be back in town in time for Thanksgiving, won't you?"

"Yes," Sharon answered after a brief hesitation. She hadn't given the holiday much thought since her emotions had been in such turmoil.

"We've missed you," her ex-mother-in-law

went on forthrightly. "You are still one of us, no matter what may be happening between you and that hardheaded son of mine, and—well— Vincent and I would be very pleased if you would join us all for dinner on Thursday."

Being invited to a family Thanksgiving at the Morellis' was probably a small thing, but Sharon was deeply moved all the same. Maria could have had her son and her grandchildren around her table on that special day without inviting an erstwhile wife, after all. "Thank you," Sharon said. "That would be nice."

"Of course, your mother is welcome, too," Maria added.

Bea had never made much of holidays, preferring to ignore them until they went away, but Sharon would extend the invitation anyway. "You realize that my presence might be awkward. Tony may not like it at all."

Maria sniffed. "Don't worry about Tonio. He'll behave himself."

In spite of everything that had happened, Sharon chuckled at Maria's motherly words.

"You get some rest," the older woman finished, "and don't worry about the children. I'll take very good care of them."

"Thank you," Sharon replied quietly, and after a few more words the two women said their farewells and hung up.

Sharon went upstairs to take a hot bath, and when that was done she crawled into bed and shivered under the covers. While she waited for sleep to overtake her, she laid plans for the morning.

It was time she stopped acting silly and made some sense of her life. She and Tony were divorced, but they had two children in common, and that meant they had to learn to talk to each other like civilized adults.

The task seemed formidable to Sharon.

12

The sound brought Sharon wide awake in an instant. She sat bolt upright in bed, her heart throbbing in her throat as she listened.

There it was again—a distinct thump. She reached out for the telephone and dialed the operator, then replaced the receiver when no one answered after nine rings. A shaky *who's there?* rose in Sharon's throat, but she couldn't get it out. Besides, she reasoned wildly, maybe it wasn't smart to let the prowler know she was there. If she kept quiet, he might steal what he wanted and leave without bothering her.

On the other hand, Sharon reflected, tossing back the covers and creeping out of bed as the noise reverberated through the A-frame again, her car was parked outside—a clear indication that someone was at home. If she just sat there with her lower lip caught between her teeth, she might end up like one of those women in the opening scenes of a horror movie.

She crept out of the bedroom and across the hall to Matt's room, where she found his baseball bat with only minimal groping. Thus armed, Sharon started cautiously down the stairs.

She'd reached the bottom when a shadow moved in the darkness. Sharon screamed and swung the bat, and something made of glass shattered.

A familiar voice rasped a swearword, and then the living room was flooded with light.

Tony was standing with his hand on the switch, looking at Sharon in weary bafflement. The mock-Tiffany lamp she'd bought at a swap meet was lying on the floor in jagged, kaleidoscope pieces.

Slowly, Sharon lowered the bat to her side. "You could have knocked," she observed lamely. Her heart was still hammering against her rib cage, and she laid one hand to her chest in an effort to calm it.

Tony was frowning. "Why would I do that when I have a key?" he asked, pulling off his jacket and tossing it onto the sofa. "Go put some shoes on, Pete Rose," he said. "I'll get the broom."

Sharon went upstairs without argument, baseball bat in hand, wanting a chance to put her thoughts into some kind of order. When she came down minutes later, she was wearing jeans, sneakers and a heavy sweater. Tony was sweeping up the last of the broken glass.

"What are you doing here?" she asked, lingering on the stairs, one hand resting on the banister.

Tony sighed. "It was Papa's idea," he said.

Sharon rolled her eyes and put her hands on her hips, mildly insulted. "Now that's romantic," she observed.

Her ex-husband disappeared with the broom and the dustpan full of glass, and when he came back there was a sheepish look about him. He went to the hearth without a word, and began building a fire.

Sharon watched him for a few moments, then went into the kitchen to heat water for coffee. Hope was pounding inside her in a strange, rising rhythm, like the beat of jungle drums. Her feelings were odd, she thought, given the number of times she and Tony had tried to find common ground and failed.

She filled the teakettle at the sink, set it on the stove and turned up the flame beneath it.

She'd just taken mugs and a jar of coffee down from the cupboard when she sensed Tony's presence and turned to see him standing in the doorway.

"I'm not going to leave," he announced with quiet resolve, "until you and I come to some kind of understanding."

Sharon sighed. "That might take a while," she answered.

He shrugged, but the expression in his eyes was anything but dispassionate. "Frankly, I've reached the point where I don't give a damn if supplies have to be airlifted in. I'm here for the duration."

The teakettle began to whistle, and Sharon took it from the heat, pouring steaming water into cups. "That's a pretty staunch position to take, considering that it was your father's idea for you to...drop in."

Tony sighed and took the cups from Sharon's hands, standing close. He set the coffee aside, and his quiet masculinity awakened all her sleepy senses. "Sharon," he said in a low voice, "I love you, and I'm pretty sure you feel the same way about me. Can't we hold on to that until we get our bearings?"

Sharon swallowed. "There are so many problems—"

"Everybody has them," he countered hoarsely. And then he took her hand in his and led her into the living room. They sat down together on the couch in front of the fireplace. Sharon, for her part, felt like a shy teenager.

"Why did you let me believe that you and Ingrid were involved?" she dared to ask. A sidelong look at Tony revealed that he was gazing into the fire.

His fingers tightened around Sharon's. The hint of a grin, rueful and brief, touched his mouth. "The answer to that should be obvious. I wanted you to be jealous."

Sharon bit her lower lip, then replied, "It worked."

Tony turned toward her then; with his free hand, he cupped her chin. "When that Swede kissed you at the party last night, I almost came out of my skin. So maybe we're even."

"Maybe," Sharon agreed with a tentative smile. She had a scary, excited feeling, as though she were setting out to cross deep waters hidden under a thin layer of ice. She was putting everything at risk, but with ever so much to be gained should she make it to the other side.

Cautiously, Tony kissed her. The fire crackled on the hearth and, in the distance, a ferry whistle made a mournful sound. After long moments of sweet anguish, he released her mouth to brush his lips along the length of her neck.

"Did your father tell you to do this, too?" Sharon asked, her voice trembling.

Tony chuckled and went right on driving her crazy. "He did suggest wine and music. I suppose he figured I could come up with the rest on my own."

Sharon closed her eyes, filled with achy yearnings. She was facing Tony now, her arms resting lightly around his neck. "Remember," she whispered, "how it used to be? When Bri was little?"

He had returned to her mouth, and sharp desire stabbed through her as he teased and tasted her. "Um-hmm. We made love on the living room floor with the stereo playing."

"Tony." The word sounded breathless and uncertain.

"What?"

"I don't see how we're going to settle anything by doing this."

She felt his smile against her lips; its warmth seemed to reach into the very depths of her being. "Let me state my position on this issue," he whispered. "I love you. I want you. And I'm not going to be able to concentrate on anything until I've had you."

Sharon trembled. "You've got your priorities in order, Morelli—I'll say that for you."

He drew her sweater up over her head and tossed it away, then unfastened her bra. Sharon drew in a sharp breath when he took both her breasts into his hands, gently chafing the nipples with the sides of his thumbs. "I'm so glad you approve," he teased gruffly, bending his head to taste her.

Sharon muffled a groan of pure pleasure and buried her fingers in his hair as he indulged. "I think—I see where we—went wrong," she managed to say. "We should never have—gotten out of bed."

Tony's chuckle felt as good against her nipple as his tongue. "Sharon?"

"What?"

"Shut up."

She moaned, arching her neck as he pressed her down onto her back and unsnapped her jeans. He left her to turn out the lights and press a button on the stereo. The room was filled with music and the gracious glow of the fire, and Tony knelt beside the sofa to caress her.

A tender delirium possessed Sharon as Tony reminded her that he knew her body almost as well as she did. There was an interval during which he drew ever greater, ever more primitive responses from her, and then he stood and lifted her into his arms. She worked the buttons on his shirt as he carried her up the stairs and into the bedroom.

The light of a November moon streamed over Tony's muscular chest and caught the tousled ebony of his hair as Sharon undressed him. In those moments she prayed to love Tony less because what she felt was too fierce and too beautiful to be endured.

He tensed as she touched one taut masculine nipple with the tip of her tongue, and she knew that the anticipation he felt was almost beyond his ability to bear. The words that fell from his lips as she pleasured him belonged not to earth but to a world that love had created, and while Sharon couldn't have defined a single one, she understood them in her heart.

When Tony had reached the limits of his control, he used gentle force to subdue Sharon; after lowering her to the bed, he clasped her wrists in his hands and stretched her arms above her head. His body, as lean and dynamic as a panther's, was poised over hers. In the icy, silver light of the moon, Sharon saw in his face both the tenderness of a lover and the hunger of a predator.

She lifted her head to kiss the curve of his collarbone. Tony could no longer restrain himself; his mouth fell to Sharon's as if he would consume her. A few hoarse, intimate words passed between them, and then, with a grace born of mutual desperation, they were joined.

Tony's and Sharon's bodies seemed to war with each other even as their souls struggled to fuse into one spirit. The skirmish began on earth and ended square in the center of heaven, and the lovers clung to each other as they drifted back to the plane where mortals belong.

When Tony collapsed beside her, still breathing hard, Sharon rolled over to look down into his face, one of her legs resting across his. She kissed the almost imperceptible cleft in his chin.

"I think my toes have melted," she confided with a contented sigh.

Tony put his arms around her, positioning her so that she lay on top of him. "Promise me something," he said, when his breathing had returned to normal. "The next time I make you mad, remember that I'm the same man who melts your toes, will you?"

Sharon kissed him. "I'll try," she said, snuggling down to lie beside Tony and wishing that this accord they'd reached would last forever. Unfortunately, they couldn't spend the rest of their lives in bed.

"What are you thinking?" Tony asked when a long time had passed. He'd turned onto his side to look into Sharon's face, and he brushed her hair away from her cheek with a gentle motion of one hand.

"That I love you. Tony, I want to make this relationship work, but I don't know how."

He sat up and reached out to turn on the lamp on the bedside table. "I've got a few theories about that."

Wriggling to an upright position, Sharon folded her arms and braced herself. She had a pretty good idea what he was going to say—that she was spreading herself too thin, that their marriage would have lasted if she hadn't insisted on opening Teddy Bares....

Tony laughed and caught her chin in his hand. "Wait a minute. I can tell by the storm clouds gathering in your eyes that you're expecting my old me-Tarzan-you-Jane routine—and I wasn't planning to do that.''

Sharon gave him a suspicious look. "Okay, so what's your theory, Morelli?''

He sighed. "That we don't fight fair. We sort of collide like bumper cars at a carnival—and then bounce off each other. I try to hurt you and you try to hurt me, and nothing ever gets settled because we're both so busy retaliating or making up that we never talk about what's really wrong.''

"That makes a scary kind of sense,'' Sharon admitted in a small voice. She couldn't look at Tony, so she concentrated on chipping the polish off the nail of her right index finger. "Where do we start?''

"With Carmen, I think,'' he said quietly.

Even after ten years as Tony's wife, after bearing one of his children and raising the other as her own, Carmen's name made Sharon feel defensive and angry. "I hate her,'' she confessed.

"I know,'' Tony replied.

Sharon made herself meet his gaze. "That's really stupid, isn't it?''

His broad, naked shoulders moved in a shrug.

"I don't know if I'd go so far as to say that. It's certainly futile."

"You loved her."

"I never denied that."

Sharon drew in a deep, shaky breath. "Even after you married me," she said, "I was a replacement for Carmen at first, wasn't I?"

He shoved a hand through his hair and, for a fraction of a second, his eyes snapped and the line of his jaw went hard. At the last moment he stopped himself from bouncing off of her like one of those carnival bumper cars he'd mentioned earlier. "It's true that I didn't take the time to work through my grief like I should have," he admitted after a long time. "The loneliness—I don't know if I can explain what it was like. It tore at me. I couldn't stand being by myself, but hanging around my family was even worse because they all seemed to have some kind of handle on their lives and I didn't."

Tentatively, Sharon reached out and took Tony's hand in hers. "Go on."

"There isn't much else to say, Sharon. I did want a wife, and I wanted a mother for Briana—but I wouldn't have had to look beyond Mama's Christmas card list for a woman to fill those roles. Mama, my aunts and sisters and female cousins—they all had prospects in mind. I married you because I wanted you.''

Sharon was watching Tony's face. ''You wanted me? Is that all?''

Tony sighed and tilted back his head, gazing forlornly up at the ceiling. ''No. I loved you, but I didn't realize it at the time. I was using you.''

This honesty business hurt. ''You—you wanted out, I suppose.''

His arm moved around her shoulders, and he drew her close. ''Never,'' he answered. ''Do you know when I figured out that I loved you as much as I'd ever loved Carmen? It was at that Fourth of July picnic when you climbed fifteen feet up a damned pine tree to get some kid's toy plane and broke your arm taking a shortcut down.''

Sharon was amazed. Her predominant memory of that first Independence Day after their marriage had been that she'd missed out on the fireworks and her share of cold watermelon because she'd spent most of the afternoon and evening in the hospital getting X rays and having a cast put on. ''That made you fall in love with me? You're a hard man to please, Morelli.''

He turned his head to kiss her temple.

''You're not listening. I said I realized that day that what I'd felt for you all along was love.''

They were silent for a few minutes, both of them lost in their own thoughts, but Sharon finally said, ''I didn't grow up in a family like yours, Tony. I didn't—and don't—have your self-confidence. My insecurities have caused a lot of problems—I can see that now.'' She paused and sighed sadly. ''And then there's Teddy Bares. How do you really feel about my business?''

''I hate it,'' he answered politely. ''But that's my problem, not yours.'' Tony scooted down far enough to give Sharon a mischievous kiss. ''I'll work through it.''

Sharon felt a quiet happiness steal through her. ''Are you saying that you want to try again?''

He cupped her breast with his hand. ''Yes,'' he answered bluntly. ''Will you give me a second chance?''

''At marriage, or our favorite nighttime activity?'' Sharon teased.

Tony began to caress her. ''Marriage. If I can dissolve your toes, lady, it would seem that I've got a handle on the rest.''

Sharon laughed, then gave a little crooning

groan as his hand moved downward to make tantalizing circles on her stomach. "It would—seem so," she agreed.

He slid beneath the covers, and his tongue encircled one of Sharon's nipples. "Marry me," he said. "Please?"

She gasped as Tony began to work his private magic. "Maybe—maybe we should live together first," she managed to say. "Until we learn to fight correctly."

"Fine," Tony agreed, preoccupied. "You explain it to Matt and Bri. And my grandmother. And—"

"I'll marry you," Sharon broke in. She pretty much knew when she was beaten. "But there will probably be a lot of fights. We'll both have to make a great many adjustments...."

"Um-hmm," Tony replied, sounding downright disinterested now. "Probably."

He was doing such delicious things to her that it was hard to speak normally. "Sometimes I'll win, and sometimes you will."

Tony flung back the covers and reached out to turn off the lamp. "I'm pretty sure you'll still be talking," he said, gathering her close to him.

He was wrong. Sharon was through talking.

* * *

When Sharon awakened the next morning, Tony wasn't in bed. She was worried for a moment until she heard him running up the stairs.

He burst into the bedroom, wearing running shorts and a tank top and dripping sweat. He gave Sharon a grin and disappeared into the bathroom to take his shower.

She waited until she heard the water come on, then went to join him.

That day was magical. They walked along the beach, hand in hand, talking, saying what they really felt, dreaming aloud and deciding how to interweave their separate hopes. They even argued at odd intervals.

It was late that night, when they were eating a complicated pasta concoction that Tony had whipped up, that the first real test of their resolve to be truthful came up.

Sharon had been talking about the opportunity she'd missed because she hadn't been able to go to Paris, and Tony said, "If you needed money, you should have asked me."

Curled up in the easy chair in front of the hearth, Sharon lowered her fork back to her plate and said quietly, "I couldn't."

Tony qualified her statement. "Because of your damned pride."

"As if you didn't have any."

A tempest was brewing in those dark, spirited eyes, but it ebbed away as fast as it had arisen, and Tony smiled, albeit sheepishly. "Okay. Back to our corners—no kidney punches and no hitting below the belt."

With a mischievous grin, Sharon set aside her plate, got out of her chair and turned the music on and the lights off. There was a nice blaze in the fireplace, and she stretched out on the floor in front of the hearth, letting the light and warmth wash over her.

When Tony joined her, she reached up and put her arms around his neck. "I've missed you so much," she said as the music swelled around them like an invisible river. Soon, it would lift them up and carry them away, and Sharon had no intention of swimming against the current. "I love you," she whispered, pulling Tony downward into her kiss.

Soon they were spinning and whirling in a torrent of sensation, and it ended with Sharon arching her back in a powerful spasm of release and crying out for Tony as she ran her hands feverishly over his flesh. He spoke tender, soothing words to her even as he tensed in the throes of his own gratification.

* * *

The big house was full of laughter and the scent of roasting turkey when Sharon and Tony arrived, and Vincent smiled when he saw them. It was Maria who took Sharon's hands in her own and thus noticed the wide golden band on her finger.

"When?" she asked, her eyes bright with joy.

Tony kissed her forehead. Before he could answer, though, Briana and Matt made their way through the crowd of cousins and aunts and uncles, approaching from different directions but arriving at the same moment.

"Something's happened," Bri said, assessing her father and then Sharon. "What is it?"

"They're married, metal-mouth," Matt told her with affectionate disdain. "Can't you see those rings they're wearing?"

Sharon nodded in answer to the hopeful question she saw shining in Bri's eyes, and the girl flung herself into her stepmother's arms with a cry of joy.

Michael, in the meantime, was shaking Tony's hand. "Does this mean you're going to be fit to work with again?" he asked, his voice gruff, his eyes shining.

Tony laughed and lifted an excited Matt into his arms.

"We're all going to live together in the same house now, right?" the little boy wanted to know.

"Right," Tony confirmed.

"How did you two manage to get a license so fast?" Tony's sister Rose demanded from somewhere in the throng of delighted relatives.

"We were married in Nevada this morning, and I chartered a plane to fly us here," he explained. "Is everybody satisfied, or do I have to call a press conference?"

Sharon got out of her coat with some help from Tony, and went into the kitchen with Maria. Bri and Rose followed.

The place was a giant cornucopia—there were pies, candied yams, special vegetable dishes, gelatin salads, cranberry sauce—all the traditional foods. Sharon wanted to help, to be a part of the festivities, and she went to the sink and started peeling the mountain of potatoes waiting there.

Maria was preparing a relish tray nearby, and Bri and Rose were arguing good-naturedly over the football game that would be played that afternoon. They weren't concerned with who would win or lose; the bone of contention was which team had the cuter players.

Within the next hour, dinner was ready to be served and Bea had arrived in her old car, proudly presenting her three-bean casserole as a contribution.

Sitting beside Tony, her hand resting in his on the tabletop, Sharon counted the men, women and children gathered to give thanks under the Morelli roof. There were forty-three smiling faces around the card tables and the oaken one that had been a part of Lucia's dowry.

A reverent prayer was said, and then Vincent began carving the first of three turkeys with great fanfare. Sharon felt the sting of happy tears in her eyes when she turned to look at Tony, then Briana, then Matt.

She offered a silent prayer of her own, one of true thanksgiving, and laughed and cheered Vincent's expertise as a turkey carver with the rest of the family.

Her family.

*   *   *   *   *

New York Times **Bestselling Author**

LINDA HOWARD

Michelle Cabot has inherited her father's Florida cattle ranch—and a mountain of debt. To make matters worse, a huge chunk of that debt is owed to her nemesis, John Rafferty. Nothing shocks Rafferty more than discovering that the pampered rich girl he once despised is trying to run the Cabot ranch herself, desperate to save the only thing she has left. What he doesn't know is that underneath Michelle's cool, polished facade lie heartache, secrets and the raw determination to live life as her own woman. But Rafferty wants her for his own...and he isn't about to take no for an answer.

HEARTBREAKER

"There is nothing quite like a sexy and suspenseful story by the amazing Linda Howard!"
—*Romantic Times*

USA Today Bestselling Author

RACHEL LEE

Deputy Sheriff Sam Canfield defied his demanding father to become a cop and marry the woman he loved, never for an instant regretting his choice. Then his wife's tragic death left him a shell of the man he once had been.

Schoolteacher Mary McKinney knows about the pain and regret that haunt Sam. The death of her son seven years ago destroyed her marriage and left her with her own sorrow and guilt. Now she wants—she *needs*—to free Sam from his demons…to help heal the rift between father and son. But in doing so, she'll put her own vulnerable heart in jeopardy.

July Thunder

"Ms. Lee tells a deeply emotional tale. As she shows a family in deep need of healing and the pain that must come before the forgiveness, she will touch readers in a very real way."
—*Romantic Times* on *A January Chill*

On sale mid-February 2002
wherever paperbacks are sold!

MIRA

If you enjoyed what you just read,
then we've got an offer you can't resist!

Take 2
bestselling novels FREE!
Plus get a FREE surprise gift!

Clip this page and mail it to The Best of the Best™

IN U.S.A.	**IN CANADA**
3010 Walden Ave.	P.O. Box 609
P.O. Box 1867	Fort Erie, Ontario
Buffalo, N.Y. 14240-1867	L2A 5X3

YES! Please send me 2 free Best of the Best™ novels and my free surprise gift. After receiving them, if I don't wish to receive anymore, I can return the shipping statement marked cancel. If I don't cancel, I will receive 4 brand-new novels every month, before they're available in stores! In the U.S.A., bill me at the bargain price of $4.24 plus 25¢ shipping and handling per book and applicable sales tax, if any*. In Canada, bill me at the bargain price of $4.74 plus 25¢ shipping and handling per book and applicable taxes**. That's the complete price and a savings of over 15% off the cover prices—what a great deal! I understand that accepting the 2 free books and gift places me under no obligation ever to buy any books. I can always return a shipment and cancel at any time. Even if I never buy another book from The Best of the Best™, the 2 free books and gift are mine to keep forever.

185 MEN DFNG
385 MEN DFNH

Name	(PLEASE PRINT)	
Address	Apt.#	
City	State/Prov.	Zip/Postal Code

* Terms and prices subject to change without notice. Sales tax applicable in N.Y.
** Canadian residents will be charged applicable provincial taxes and GST.
  All orders subject to approval. Offer limited to one per household and not valid to current Best of the Best™ subscribers.
  ® are registered trademarks of Harlequin Enterprises Limited.

B0B01
©1998 Harlequin Enterprises Limited